very still &
hard to see

by Steve Yockey

A Samuel French Acting Edition

SAMUEL FRENCH

FOUNDED 1830

SAMUELFRENCH.COM

ISBN 978-0-573-70055-2   Printed in U.S.A.   #20361

MUSIC USE NOTE

Licensees are solely responsible for obtaining formal written permission from copyright owners to use copyrighted music in the performance of this play and are strongly cautioned to do so. If no such permission is obtained by the licensee, then the licensee must use only original music that the licensee owns and controls. Licensees are solely responsible and liable for all music clearances and shall indemnify the copyright owners of the play and their licensing agent, Samuel French, Inc., against any costs, expenses, losses and liabilities arising from the use of music by licensees.

IMPORTANT BILLING AND CREDIT
REQUIREMENTS

All producers of *VERY STILL & HARD TO SEE must* give credit to the Author of the Play in all programs distributed in connection with performances of the Play, and in all instances in which the title of the Play appears for the purposes of advertising, publicizing or otherwise exploiting the Play and/or a production. The name of the Author *must* appear on a separate line on which no other name appears, immediately following the title and *must* appear in size of type not less than fifty percent of the size of the title type.

foolish heart was commissioned by South Coast Repertory in Costa Mesa, CA. It premiered as a part of the *Car Plays* in the Segerstrom Center for the Arts *Off Center Festival* on January 14, 2012. Directed by Ron Klier. With the following cast:

MINDY	Jennifer Christopher
KEITH	Johnny Clark

heavy cream was commissioned and produced by Southern Rep in New Orleans, LA. It premiered on October 28, 2010 at the Le Chat Noir Theatre as a part of *GoodNight*. Directed by Aimee Hayes. With the following cast:

ADAM	Sean Glazebrook
SALLY	Robin Baudier
JAMES	James Bartelle
BETTY	Aimee Hayes

[epistolary] was commissioned by the Dept of Theatre, Performance Studies, and Dance at Kennesaw State University in Atlanta, GA. It premiered as a part of "*What's Your Secret?*" *Inspired by PostSecret* on October 5, 2010. Directed by Margaret Baldwin. With the following cast:

KATE	Tori Bennett
LINDSAY	Tara Parker
SAMMY	Rachel DuJulio
SARAH (A)	Minoo Bassery
SARAH (B)	Blaire Hillman

hysterical: a play that tastes like black licorice was commissioned and produced by Dad's Garage in Atlanta, GA. It opened on July 10, 2009 as a part of *Fingertips*. Directed by Matthew Meyers. With the following cast:

ELIZABETH	Amber Nash
WHITE STAG	Rene Dellefont

lucky was commissioned by Marin Theatre Company in Mill Valley, CA. It premiered on May 5, 2012 as a part of their 45th Anniversary Gala. Developed from an initial idea prompt by Elizabeth Banks. Directed by Margot Melcon. With the following cast:

"PONY" SMITH	Patrick Russell
WHISKEY BARREL	Dan Hiatt
BICYCLE BELL	Anna Bullard

bedtime was commissioned and produced by Southern Rep in New Orleans, LA. It premiered on October 28, 2010 at the Le Chat Noir Theatre as a part of *GoodNight*. Directed by Aimee Hayes. With the following cast:

VIOLET	Becca Chapman
JULIE	Robin Baudier
BAG MAN	Matt Stanley

a lovely violent ghost haiku with gun was commissioned and produced by Southern Rep in New Orleans, LA. It premiered on October 28, 2010 at the Le Chat Noir Theatre as a part of *GoodNight*. Directed by Aimee Hayes. With the following cast:

BOY . . . . Matt Standley
GIRL . . . . Becca Chapman

wallpaper was commissioned and produced by Southern Rep in New Orleans, LA. It premiered on October 28, 2010 at the Le Chat Noir Theatre as a part of *GoodNight*. Directed by Aimee Hayes. With the following cast:

LINDSAY . . . . Becca Chapman
WOMAN. . . . . Robin Baudier

when it happens it will happen quietly was commissioned by Dominic D'Andrea for the Los Angeles One Minute Play Festival. It appeared on November 17, 2011 as a part of Cornerstone Theater Company's *Creative Seeds: An Exploration of Hunger* project. Directed by Ashley Teague. With the following cast:

KITH . . . . Gabriel Rodriguez
KIN . . . . Paula Weston Solano

very still & hard to see was commissioned by Melissa Y. Smith for the American Conservatory Theatre graduate acting company. It opened in workshop on December 7, 2011 in the Hastings Studio Theater. Directed by Melissa Y. Smith and Stephen Buescher, with production design by Mark Robinson, and Workshop Stage Manager by Christina Hogan. With the following (expanded) cast:

OBAKE	Elyse Price
BUCK	Philip Estrera
JASPER	Aaron Moreland
BETTY	Lisa Kitchens
ETHAN	Asher Grodman
EDITH	Lateefah Holder
GINGER	Blair Busbee
FRANKLIN	Dillon Heape
SIMONE	Nemuna Ceesay
DAVID	York Walker

very still & hard to see was produced by The Production Company in Los Angeles, CA on June 1, 2012 at The Lex. Producers were August Viverito and T.L. Kolman. Directed by Michael Matthews, with assistant direction by Jen Albert, lighting by Tim Swiss, sound by Cricket Myers, and property design by Michael O'Hara. With the following cast:

OBAKE	CB Spencer
BUCK	Andrew Crabtree
ETHAN	James Louis Wagner
BETTY	Katherine Skelton
EDITH	Adeye Sahran
GINGER	Tiffany Cole
FRANKLIN	Coleman Drew
DAVID	Michael Tauzin

CONTENTS

foolish heart

LIST OF PLAYERS

MINDY: a woman, a wife, "type A" and one for making plans, but not always good plans

KEITH: a man, a husband, in love with Mindy but it's not easy trying to go along with this program

NOTES

[ ] in the script indicate overlapping dialogue.

The play is realism and definitely reaches a pretty raw place but it tilts intentionally towards melodrama by virtue of the stakes alone. That should be acknowledged and embraced.

The action takes place in the front seat of a parked car.

(The slamming of the trunk shakes the car.)

(Suddenly **KEITH** *jumps into the driver's seat and* **MINDY** *jumps into the passenger seat, slamming the door. She has a plastic bag of some kind and it smells acutely antiseptic.)*

(They are both a bit disheveled and breathing heavy. They do not speak for a while. He looks at her a few times. She never looks back. Then all at once...)

KEITH. What the fuck, Mindy, I mean, seriously, what the fuck were you thinking and, just, you said you wanted me to meet him, meet him, you said you wanted, holy fuck, this is not what we talked about and what are you doing, are you listening, are you [even fucking...]

(Without looking at him, **MINDY** *holds up her hand sharply...)*

MINDY. [Just...!]

(Pause. He waits. She suddenly pulls down the passenger side visor to get at the mirror. She brushes her hair out of the way and checks her face.)

KEITH. What are you doing?!

MINDY. I'm going to have a bruise.

KEITH. He kicked you in the face.

MINDY. Oh, Keith, he didn't mean to.

KEITH. Yes he did, he did mean to; he didn't want to go with [us, Mindy.]

MINDY. [He doesn't] know any [better.]

KEITH. [What did you] even, how long is he going to be out like that?

MINDY. I don't know, an hour?

KEITH. You don't know?

MINDY. An hour or so, that's what it said online, I don't [know, an hour.]

KEITH. [Ugh, it smells] sweet, what is that?

(**MINDY** *ties off the plastic bag and throws it on the floorboard.*)

MINDY. I got it from Nancy Bell.

KEITH. Nancy from the dentist office?

MINDY. He's going to be fine in no [time, you'll see.]

KEITH. [You could have] really hurt him!

MINDY. I'm saving him.

KEITH. You put him in the trunk.

MINDY. This is what good parents do [for their kids.]

KEITH. [He's unconscious] in the trunk.

MINDY. I'm bringing him home!

KEITH. Listen to yourself! You knocked out some helpless little boy with, what? Chloroform? Was it Chloroform? To keep him safe?! And now he's in the trunk [of our car!]

MINDY. [Stop yelling,] I did what I had to do [and I...]

KEITH. [That is so] [far beyond...]

MINDY. [And I didn't] tell you about it because you would have tried to stop me.

KEITH. I didn't realize what you were doing until it [was done.]

MINDY. [And that] was the plan!

KEITH. I can't believe this, I'm not, I'm not doing this, Mindy. I'm not. Jesus, I know you're sad, but [this is insane.]

MINDY. [Sad? Sad?!] That's it right there, Keith. You've never understood, ever. Ever. And [it's not...]

KEITH. [Don't you say that] to me. Don't. You. Dare.

(*pause*)

MINDY. I didn't mean that.

KEITH. Yes, you did.

MINDY. I just, I don't know [how to…]

KEITH. [I never] should have, when we started coming to this playground. When you started watching him in particular. Who comes to a playground every night at dusk to watch other people's children? Who does that? I shouldn't have humored you, but it seemed to make you so happy. I never imagined that [it would…]

MINDY. [Humored] me?

(He turns on her.)

KEITH. It's not him.

MINDY. Look at his hair, look at his eyes, look at his fucking eyes.

KEITH. He has brown eyes, a lot of kids have brown eyes, a lot of people have [brown eyes.]

MINDY. [No, it's] him. It is, you just can't accept it yet. Give it time and [you'll see.]

KEITH. [We're not] going to give it time.

MINDY. I'm not watching him go home with those other people one more night, Keith. I absolutely will not. Now start the car. No one saw us, somehow no one saw us, so start the car and let's go home. Let's go home and it will be home again because our whole family will be there. All of us. Doesn't that sound amazing? Doesn't that sound perfect? I know you want it as much as I do, that's why you didn't stop me from putting him in the trunk. You do see it, see him. They were wrong when they told us what happened, they were wrong and he's been growing up with other, with those "people" and now we've got him back. Start. The. Car.

*(Pause. **KEITH** puts his hands on the keys and exhales. Then he looks at her as he tears up…)*

KEITH. It's not Billy.

MINDY. Did you really [look at…?]

KEITH. [It's not] Billy.

MINDY. He's the right age; he looks [just like…]

KEITH. [It's not] Billy.

MINDY. Stop it!

KEITH. Billy's dead, Mindy.

(**MINDY** *looks horrified.*)

I know you don't want me to say it and you don't want to hear it, but Billy's dead, he isn't [coming back.]

MINDY. [Stop it! Stop it,] stop it!

(**MINDY** *slaps* **KEITH.** *She slaps him again and again and begins hitting him. She loses control, crying and hitting.* **KEITH** *blocks his face, but makes no effort to stop her. He just keeps quietly repeating...*)

KEITH. I'm sorry.

(*Eventually, and this may take a while,* **MINDY** *stops. She leans against him, breathing heavy.*)

MINDY. I have no idea what I'm doing, Keith.

(**KEITH** *puts his arm around her and she hides her face in his chest.*)

KEITH. I know.

MINDY. Is it Billy?

KEITH. No.

MINDY. It feels like...it has to be. Oh god.

(*He holds her. After a moment, he begins to hum and then sing the Steve Perry's 1984 hit "Foolish Heart." Very quietly. It is absolutely intimate and only for her. He sings as much of it as he needs to...*)

KEITH. "Feelin' that feelin' again
    I'm playin' a game I can't win
    Love's knockin' on the door
    Of my heart once more
    Think I'll let her in
    Before I begin

KEITH. *(cont.)* Foolish Heart
    Hear me callin'

Stop before
You start fallin'
Foolish heart
Heed my warnin'
You've been wrong before
Don't be wrong anymore
Foolish heart"

(**MINDY** *manages to pull it together a bit. She's trying.*)

MINDY. You never sing anymore.

KEITH. I know.

MINDY. We used to dance to that song.

KEITH. Well, it's our song. And we can still dance to it.

MINDY. I don't feel like I could ever dance again.

KEITH. There are all kinds of things we can still do, will still do, Mindy. I promise.

(*He pushes her back so they're facing each other and brushes the hair out of her face.*)

But if we don't stop this now, if we do this thing, then it'll be the only thing we ever do again. We will live it every day, every single day, until we get caught or can't do it anymore or until one day that little boy grows up and asks us why we would do this. And I can't look back at him and say, "Because we were sad." Yell at me all you want, Mindy, I know you don't like that word or you think it's too small? But that's what we are now. Sad. Deeply, achingly sad. And this will not make it better.

(**MINDY** *begins crying again.*)

MINDY. I miss him so much.

KEITH. I do, too.

MINDY. It's not fair.

KEITH. You're right. But that doesn't mean we can replace him.

MINDY. I wasn't trying to, I [would never...]

KEITH. [It doesn't] mean that we can put some other family through what we've gone through. We can't, Mindy. We won't.

MINDY. I didn't…think of that.

KEITH. We have to get out of the car, open the trunk and get some help for that boy. All right? We have to stop this right now.

MINDY. All right.

KEITH. All right?

MINDY. I don't…yes.

KEITH. We're going to be in trouble. I'll say it was me, all right?

MINDY. No.

KEITH. I'll explain it [to them.]

MINDY. [You don't] have [to do that.]

KEITH. [They'll believe] me, believe that and, maybe, I'm saying maybe, maybe for a second I thought…maybe I didn't stop you because I…

(She looks at him with all of the hope in the world in her eyes. He tears up and smiles at her, but then shakes his head "no.")

MINDY. He does look like Billy.

KEITH. He does.

MINDY. It's lovely, isn't it?

*(**KEITH** shakes it off. He pops the trunk.)*

*(He gets out of the car and closes the door. He walks around the back of the car and can be heard moving something in the trunk. **MINDY** checks herself in the mirror again, takes a deep breath, and gets out of the car. The door slams. The trunk slams.)*

End of Play

heavy cream

LIST OF PLAYERS

ADAM: a frustrated business man showing the signs of sleep deprivation.

SALLY: a very put together woman, all business with a clear eye for advancement

JAMES: an optimistic man, probably not very well cut out for management.

BETTY: a young woman, a Buttercow Milk Page in a white fitted skirt, white blouse and a little white bellhop hat, red heels, red lips. She has an enormous bundle of a white balloons.

NOTES

[ ] in the script indicate overlapping dialogue.

The play is divided into 3 parts and should ideally be broken up throughout an evening of plays.

heavy cream (part 1)

(JAMES, ADAM and SALLY stand in an empty room.)

(They have nametags and are dressed for work. Business casual. They stand waiting.)

(The only other items in the room are a bottle of milk and a hammer sitting on top of a stool.)

SALLY. Hmm. Adam? Milk and a hammer.

JAMES. And a stool.

SALLY. I thought there'd be more up here; this is just an empty room.

ADAM. I'm sure it's just a waiting room of some kind.

SALLY. It doesn't feel like a waiting room; there's nowhere to sit.

JAMES. You could sit on the stool?

ADAM. Don't touch anything.

JAMES. Maybe it's more of a "holding" room.

ADAM. Just shut-up, James. Why did they insist on meeting so late?

SALLY. Would you please stop complaining. If you embarrass me in front of the upper management, I will punch you in the face. We're a team, all three of us, in fact we're the best god damn sales team 3 months running and someone up here finally noticed. So don't fuck it up.

ADAM. You're not the boss, Sally. Even when you act like you are.

JAMES. I'm sure I could just move the milk and the hammer.

SALLY. Ugh. Shut-up, James.

(Pause. Then JAMES crosses over to the milk and touches the bottle.)

19

ADAM. I said don't touch anything!

JAMES. Wow. The bottle is really cold. And it's not milk, it's…

*(Suddenly **SALLY** enters. She is in a white fitted skirt, white blouse and a little white bellhop hat. Her heels are red. He lipstick is red. She holds a large bundle of a white balloons.)*

BETTY. Sorry to keep you waiting. I'm Betty, one of the Buttercow Dairy Company executive pages. We all dress the same, so it's all right if you mix us up. You could say we work for the big cheese. You could say that, but no one would laugh. Trust me. Oh, you might be wondering about these balloons. Me too. What am I even doing with these balloons? No ideas? All right, I thought maybe you would know. Anyhoo, everything you'll need for the executive assessment is in this room. I've been told to tell you that the test starts now and the higher ups will be watching.

ADAM. There must be some mistake.

SALLY. We're here because our team has been on top for the past 3 months.

BETTY. That's right. No mistake. Well, these heels might be a mistake by the end of today, we'll see. They're a little snug. Anyhoo, only one of you gets the promotion. Let's see: stool, hammer, bottle of Buttercow heavy cream, yes, everything's right here. So…best of luck.

*(**BETTY** exits. **ADAM**, **SALLY** and **JAMES** exchange nervous looks.)*

End Part 1

heavy cream (part 2)

(JAMES, ADAM and SALLY are sitting on the floor. JILL's shoes are off and ADAM has rolled up his sleeves.)

JILL. Do you think she's coming back? Ever?

ADAM. Hopefully someone else is coming back instead. That other lady with the balloons didn't seem to have a very clear idea of why we're up here.

JAMES. Her name is Betty.

ADAM. Do I give a fuck, James? She's a page. And she left us sitting here.

JAMES. Never hurts to be nice. Look, I don't want to sit on the floor anymore, I'm sitting on the stool.

(He crosses over and pointedly moves the milk bottle and hammer to the floor. He looks at ADAM and JILL and then sits on the stool.)

JILL. You can't just put things on the floor.

JAMES. You two are just exceptionally pleasant.

JILL & ADAM. Shut-up, James.

(BETTY enters again. The Balloons are gone.)

BETTY. Hello again. Just checking your progress. Hmmm. Oh, the balloons were for the champagne toast. There's a champagne toast for whoever gets the promotion, right outside there. Everyone's waiting so tick tock, you know? Like the sound of a clock ticking. As in if you could move this along, that'd be just swell. I mean, it's almost midnight.

ADAM. It's been 5 hours?

JILL. A simple misunderstanding, I'm sure. It's just, I'm afraid that no one's explained the, um, the "process" exactly? Was there maybe a memo we were meant to receive down on seven?

BETTY. Stool, hammer, bottle of Buttercow heavy cream. Only one of you leaves the room.

JAMES. Leaves the room?

BETTY. Mm hm. Oh, only one of you gets the job. That's all the explanation that any of the other teams have needed. And they caught on a lot faster, although I shouldn't say so. I could ask one of the executives if you'd like? But Buttercow Dairy Company is one of the oldest and most successful providers of dairy products in the world, so I'd think that their human resource policies must be fairly effective. The pages all have to learn the complete company history. Anyhoo, did you want me to ask someone?

JILL. No, no. No need to tell anyone anything. We'll just…

(She gestures to the milk bottle and the hammer. **JAMES** *hops off the stool reflexively.)*

JAMES. Sorry.

JILL. I'm sure we'll figure it out.

BETTY. That's so great. I'll let them know.

*(***BETTY*** exits. They all sit for a moment.)*

ADAM. Fuck.

End Part 2

heavy cream (part 3)

(**ADAM** *sits on the floor, head in hands.* **SALLY** *rests her head against the wall.* **JAMES** *is back on the stool finishing off the last of the heavy cream in the bottle.* **SALLY** *notices.*)

JAMES. I was hungry.

SALLY. You don't drink heavy cream.

JAMES. It's been hours. I didn't have lunch.

ADAM. What if we were hungry, too?

JAMES. Were you going to drink heavy cream?

ADAM. No.

JILL. Not a chance.

JAMES. So then there's no issue. Go team.

JILL. What team? If you two would just acknowledge that I'm the reason our team is so successful, then we wouldn't even need to go through this.

ADAM. First off, no you're not. Second, what about this situation makes you think you wouldn't have to complete this, whatever it is, test or task or, what makes you think if we threw our hands up you'd get the job?

JILL. Because it demonstrates my superiority and "go getter" attitude.

ADAM. You sound ridiculous. My wife and I are up to our eyeballs in this mortgage. I'm the only one here with a family to support. That might not be fair, but it's true. So you can forget about that little plan. I'm getting this promotion. The clients like me better than you anyway. Because they can tell you're a bitch.

JILL. Huh. Okay.

JAMES. Come on, you two. Can we not, please?

(While **JAMES** *is talking,* **JILL** *moves. In one motion,* **JILL** *crosses over, picks up the hammer. Walks over to* **ADAM** *and hits him in the shin. Hard. He screams out and falls to the ground.)*

ADAM. Holy shit, argh, I think you broke my shin.

JILL. I don't think you can break your shin, Adam.

ADAM. Of fucking course you can!!

JAMES. Have you lost your [mind?]

JILL. [Shut-the-fuck]-up, James! And you, family man, unless you want me to keep hitting you then you should rethink your stance on this promotion.

*(***ADAM*** looks at her like she's crazy. She hits his leg again. He screams.)*

They left this here for a reason, Adam!

ADAM. Okay! Okay okay, you can have the fucking job!

(He holds his leg in pain, eyes closed tight. **JILL** *turns on* **JAMES.***)*

JAMES. Stay the fuck away from me.

JILL. Just say that I'm the one that deserves the promotion and you doge the hammer, James.

(She takes a step towards him. He throws the stool at her. She stumbles back and trips over **ADAM***'s leg, causing him to scream again.* **JILL** *falls, dropping the hammer.* **ADAM** *grabs it and hits her in the arm. She cries out.)*

What is wrong with you?!?!

ADAM. Me?

*(***BETTY*** enters.* **ADAM***,* **JILL** *and* **JAMES** *stop and look at her.)*

BETTY. Just checking in. Oh my!

JILL. We're working it out.

ADAM. This is fucking bullshit.

BETTY. I see the stool. Clearly there's the hammer. Who drank the heavy cream?

JAMES. I did. I hope that was okay?

ADAM. God damn it.

JILL. Wc told him not to touch it.

JAMES. I didn't have lunch today and my head was starting to hurt. If it impacts the team, it's totally my fault.

BETTY. You drank all of it?

(JAMES looks at ADAM and JILL, then back to BETTY.)

JAMES. Yes.

BETTY. Good. Brand loyalty is so important, don't you think. People have to believe you love the product enough to use it yourself. Come with me.

(BETTY takes JAMES by the arm and begins to lead him out. He looks over his shoulder at JILL and ADAM on the floor. BETTY notices.)

You'd be amazed how often this exact same thing happens. Sometimes even bloodier. Sometimes we need a clean up team. Anyhoo, we'll laugh about it later. Maybe not laugh. But definitely grin in a very private victory.

(JAMES looks at JILL and ADAM for a moment. Then he smiles.)

JAMES. Good night.

JILL. Fuck you!

(They exit. JILL and ADAM are stunned. And alone.)

End

[epistolary]

LIST OF PLAYERS

KATE: a lovelorn young woman

LINDSAY: a nosey young woman

SAMMY: a woman trying to explain

SARAH (a): a spurned lover; an object of affection

SARAH (b): a spurned lover; an object of affection

NOTES

[ ] in the script indicate overlapping dialogue.

A secret inside of a letter inside of a letter inside of a letter

The framing scene with Lindsay & Kate and Sammy's stand-alone monologues are behind a "fourth wall" convention. The raucous, overlapping Sarah section is direct address to the audience; very isolated, stark, think "Brechtian."

Sarah (a) and Sarah (b) are essentially the same character. As if the paper has been folded over the letter has copied onto itself.

(Lights up on LINDSAY. She is reading a letter and smiling. She sits next to a pillow. Her hand is on her heart. At one point, she moves it to her mouth because the content of the letter is so moving. Then KATE enters. She stops when she sees LINDSAY and drops her bag, almost reflexively.)

(LINDSAY immediately tries to shove the letter back in an envelope and shove it under the pillow. But clearly this takes too long to cover anything at all.)

KATE. What are you doing in my room?

LINDSAY. Hi, Kate. Hey.

KATE. Hey. Hi. Hello. What are you [doing?]

LINDSAY. [Nothing.]

KATE. Lindsay.

LINDSAY. Reading.

KATE. Reading what?

LINDSAY. A private letter of yours that you were hiding under your pillow that I didn't mean to find and really didn't mean to read.

(pause)

KATE. Huh.

LINDSAY. I'm so sorry.

KATE. Uh huh.

LINDSAY. I was just waiting for you to get ready and there's no where in room to sit except the bed and there it was sticking out from under the pillow and I know it was none of my business but you know how I am with secrets so I just [kind of...]

KATE. [Read it.]

LINDSAY. It's so beautiful. Well, the part I read. I only read the first [part.]

29

KATE. [It is] beautiful. And it's private.

LINDSAY. I said I was sorry.

KATE. That actually doesn't sound like an apology.

LINDSAY. Well, I don't, I can't unread it.

KATE. Ugh, it's fine. Are you ready to go?

LINDSAY. Yes, but can…okay, could I read the rest of it? I know, I completely know, don't make that face, I just really want to know the rest of it. Or is that…?

(**LINDSAY** *looks at her. She then throws her hands up and crosses over to the pillow. She pulls the letter out from under it, rips it out of the envelope and holds the paper up.*)

KATE. Ready?

LINDSAY. Yes, please.

(**KATE** *sighs.*)

KATE. I really can't believe you sometimes.

(*She begins to read. Lights up on* **SAMMY**. *She is kneeling and holding a small, delicate origami crane. She examines it as she begins…*)

SAMMY. I don't know what to say. I found the most amazing thing. That's not why I'm writing you, but I'm stalling, I guess, before I get to the point. I found this origami bird, but it has note on the inside. And because of how the paper was folded, the printing has doubled over on itself, so the beginning is kind of echoed over the end. It's hard to read, but still worth the effort. And it got me thinking that I should apologize. And then I started thinking about holding this little paper animal. And then I started thinking about you holding me. It's funny, when you hold me, when I imagine what that's like. Not when you hold me, how you hold me, but more how it feels. I feel your arms around me, and you tighten a bit, do you know you do that? You linger and there's a little squeeze, subtle, and I feel myself closing in. Like I'm so small. No, it's not a feeling, I am, I am so small that I could just fit in the palm of your hand, right in the middle, resting, waiting. Even when we're fighting, even when things are as bad as they maybe seem right now, some secret thing, all angles and edges. And you can, I mean, if you want to, you can unfold me. But you have to be careful, a little bit at a time. I have all of these secrets for you.

(As **SAMMY** *begins to slowly unfold the paper crane, lights rise on* **SARAH** (a) *and* **SARAH** (b), *both facing the audience.* **SARAH** (a) *holds her left palm open and holds a tangled piece of twine.* **SARAH** (b) *has her fists closed; she is crushing a piece of twine in her left fist.)*

SARAH (b). And I'll be smiling. So I hope you're ready. Love, Sarah.

SARAH (a). Hey, I've been trying to find reasons not to write this. I actually just tried to untie this stupid twine someone left it in the hall, all tied up in knots. A perfectly good piece of twine. That's how much I wanted to avoid this.

SARAH (b). And you'll lie there bleeding, maybe crying in pain, if you're even somehow conscious.

SARAH (a). I'm sure it's still good, if I can just get it untied. I really can't imagine why someone would just leave it here.

SARAH (b). Right through you your worthless heart.

SARAH (a). Anyway, I'll get it untied. And then I'll…well, I don't know. I don't even know what I'll do with it really, how silly.

SARAH (b). Like I pointed a rusty old cannon right at your chest and lit the fucking fuse. There'll be a smoking hole, perfectly round, right through you.

*(***SARAH** (A) *closes her hand on the twine and lets it fall to her side.)*

SARAH (a). Anyway, thanks for reading this. I realize this could be a little awkward after everything.

SARAH (b). Like getting hit in the chest with something heavy. And hard.

SARAH (a). You looked good [when I saw you.]

SARAH (b). [You fucking better…]

SARAH (a). It's about time we tried to talk about this, you know?

SARAH (b). [You think you're ready for that?]

SARAH (a). [You think you're ready for that?]

SARAH (b). That's right.

SARAH (a). However it seems maybe to you, I can kinda' explain because it can't really be ending, I mean it's not going to just end.

SARAH (b). You know, the next time I see you, I can't even, I swear I will do something awful to you. And it won't be something you'll get over, it'll hurt and it'll knock you the fuck back. Leave you dizzy and stunned.

SARAH (a). It wasn't a smart thing to do; it was the wrong thing to do. I'm not trying to explain it. I just want you to know it didn't mean anything.

SARAH (b). Fuck you.

SARAH (a). [You don't even look at me anymore.]

SARAH (b). [I can't even look at you anymore!]

SARAH (a). Seriously, we can't, we're both just gonna' keep doing this over and over.

SARAH (b). Fine! So I cheated on you, you cheated on me; you slept with almost everyone we've ever known to get back at me. Does it feel good?

SARAH (a). I know you still love me. And I can change okay? I mean I can be whatever I need to, whatever you want.

SARAH (b). I don't want to get into this again, but I will.

SARAH (a). [You don't want to hear this.]

SARAH (b). [I really can't believe this!]

SARAH (a). [[God dammit! All we do is go round and round. It's fucking ridiculous. And it's never going to get better, even writing this now I know that.]]

SARAH (b). [[God dammit! All we do is go round and round. It's fucking ridiculous. And it's never going to get better, even writing this now I know that.]]

SARAH (a). [I really can't believe this!]

SARAH (b). [You don't want to hear this.]

SARAH (a). I don't want to get into this again, but I will.

SARAH (b). I know you still love me. And I can change okay? I mean I can be whatever I need to, whatever you want.

SARAH (a). Fine! So I cheated on you, you cheated on me; you slept with almost everyone we've ever known to get back at me. Does it feel good?

SARAH (b). Seriously, we can't, we're both just gonna' keep doing this over and over.

SARAH (a). [I can't even look at you anymore!]

SARAH (b). [You don't even look at me anymore.]

SARAH (a). Fuck you.

SARAH (b). It wasn't a smart thing to do; it was the wrong thing to do. I'm not trying to explain it. I just want you to know it didn't mean anything.

SARAH (a). You know, the next time I see you, I can't even, I swear I will do something awful to you. And it won't be something you'll get over, it'll hurt and it'll knock you the fuck back. Leave you dizzy and stunned.

SARAH (b). However it seems maybe to you, I can kinda' explain because it can't really be ending, I mean it's not going to just end.

SARAH (a). That's right.

SARAH (b). [You think you're ready for that?]

SARAH (a). [You think you're ready for that?]

SARAH (b). It's about time we tried to talk about this, you know?

SARAH (a). [You fucking better…]

SARAH (b). [You looked good] when I saw you.

SARAH (a). Like getting hit in the chest with something heavy. And hard.

SARAH (b). Anyway, thanks for reading this. I realize this could be a little awkward after everything.

(SARAH (b) opens her palm, presenting the piece of twine.)

SARAH (a). Like I pointed a rusty old cannon right at your chest and lit the fucking fuse. There'll be a smoking hole, perfectly round, right through you.

SARAH (b). Anyway, I'll get it untied. And then I'll…well, I don't know. I don't even know what I'll do with it really, how silly.

SARAH (a). Right through you your worthless heart.

SARAH (b). I'm sure it's still good, if I can just get it untied. I really can't imagine why someone would just leave it here.

SARAH (a). And you'll lie there bleeding, maybe crying in pain, if you're even somehow conscious.

SARAH (b). Hey, I've been trying to find reasons not to write this. I actually just tried to untie this stupid twine someone left it in the hall, all tied up in knots. A perfectly good piece of twine. That's how much I wanted to avoid this.

SARAH (a). And I'll be smiling. So I hope you're ready. Love Sarah.

*(Lights dim on **SARAH** (a) and **SARAH** (b). **SAMMY** now has unfolded the piece of paper and smoothed it out on the floor.)*

SAMMY. All of these secrets are written on every little side, every piece that's exposed. Things you can't even imagine. Everyone has those things, secrets I mean, but mine are here, right here where you can read every one. One fold at a time, just like this note on the inside of a paper bird. But be careful when you unfold me, careful not to tear me, not to crush me, smudge me. Because I'm very small, when I'm with you, I can't be anything but small. Which is maybe why I get scared sometimes and get upset sometimes. And maybe over-react. And maybe have to apologize again. It's just that once you unfold me, I'm not a little paper animal any-more. That fades away as you find out more and more until I'm not anything but writing on a piece of paper. Just a piece of paper and then that fades too. Then I'm not anything but what you think of what's written there, so much smaller than you can even imagine, in your eyes, in your arms, that's what happens...every time. It's hard to put into words. But these are the ones I found. I'm sorry. And I love you. Sammy.

(Lights dim on **SAMMY**.*)*

LINDSAY. It's so romantic. And sad and sweet and, somehow, hopeful. You're lucky.

KATE. What?

LINDSAY. You're so lucky that someone would send you that.

KATE. No. No, this isn't...I found this crushed between some pages of a copy of *The Tale of Genji* in the library.

LINDSAY. Oh.

KATE. Right? Not exactly a romance novel. Or even a novel, really.

LINDSAY. And you're keeping it under your, I mean, that's not strange or anything, but why are you hanging on to it?

KATE. I just...I'd like to get something like this someday. A real love letter. From someone actually in love with me. I know how that sounds, but [it's why...]

LINDSAY. [I understand.]

KATE. Do you?

LINDSAY. Who doesn't want that?

KATE. I guess. It's still embarrassing that you found it.

LINDSAY. Also, I think Sammy might've been a girl anyway. Probably writing to a boy. Ostensibly.

KATE. *(laughing)* I don't care. For that kind of love? I'd almost rather it be a girl anyway.

LINDSAY. Ah.

KATE. That's not, oh, is that weird?

LINDSAY. No. Not at all.

KATE. I kinda' thought you knew that. About me.

LINDSAY. Maybe, but I didn't know you wanted me to know that about you.

KATE. Well, now you know.

(*pause*)

LINDSAY. I could…I mean, I can write you a letter if you want?

KATE. A love letter?

LINDSAY. You deserve to have something like that written for you. I think.

KATE. Because you feel bad for me.

LINDSAY. No.

(*They look at each other.* LINDSAY *smiles.*)

KATE. Oh.

LINDSAY. So I'll write you one.

KATE. Okay.

LINDSAY. And it'll be better than that.

(**KATE** *smiles to herself, a bit bashful.*)

KATE. Soon?

End of Play

hysterical

a play that tastes like black licorice

LIST OF PLAYERS

ELIZABETH: a woman in her 20s with a penchant for strong alcohol and suppressing both her feelings and reality.

WHITE STAG: A white stag with impressive antlers. Theoretically there would be a glowing white cross floating above his head, but probably not.

NOTES ON STAGING

[ ] indicate overlapping dialogue.

The White Stag can be a guy in jeans and a white t-shirt with giant antlers, a puppet maybe or, if available, an actual giant White Stag with a glowing cross.

Once things get rolling, they roll downhill quickly. Just like drinking, it can really get messy.

(ELIZABETH stands alone on stage. She has a bottle of Jägermeister in one hand, a shot glass in the other. A stool or small table sits just to the side.)

ELIZABETH. This is Jägermeister.

(She opens the bottle, pours a shot and knocks it back. She places the bottle and glass down on the table. She's probably already had a few...)

Master hunter, that's what it means, in German I mean, master hunter. This is my favorite drink right now. This is my absolute favorite: the taste, the kick. That kick, I mean, right? I like that after a few sips I don't have to think about anything that I don't want to think about. I don't have to think about anything at all. I don't even have to think about my ex-boyfriend after I drink enough of it. I like that a lot. I even like the taste. Black licorice. Or at least that's what I imagine it tastes like because you don't really taste it after the few sips. I keep saying sips, that's not what I mean.

(She knocks back another shot.)

But, I mean, the bottle's a little dramatic, right? I happen to find the idea of a giant white stag wandering through the woods with a big glowing cross floating between his antlers pretty ridiculous. Or creepy. But mostly ridiculous.

(The WHITE STAG enters. ELIZABETH turns and sees him.)

Okay. That's not cool. Anyway, I do like this little thing on the label, this phrase? It's in German too, but it basically says: "It's the hunter's honor to protect and preserve his game, to hunt sportsmanlike and to honor the Creator," and that's, ostensibly, that's God or something. The Creator I mean, "to honor the Creator in his creatures."

(She looks over her shoulder at the **WHITE STAG.** *She looks back at the audience.)*

ELIZABETH. *(cont.)* You see that too, right?

WHITE STAG. It sounds better in German.

ELIZABETH. Perfect. It talks.

WHITE STAG. It sounds better like this:

(An eerie green light reminiscent of the glass of a Jägermeister bottle illuminates the **WHITE STAG** *as he recites the slogan. It fades as he finishes up.)*

"Das ist des Jägers Ehrenschild, dass er beschützt und hegt sein Wild, weidmännisch jagt, wie sich's gehört, den Schöpfer im Geschöpfe ehrt."

ELIZABETH. Shut-up.

WHITE STAG. How many of those have you had?

ELIZABETH. Shut-up.

WHITE STAG. Right.

ELIZABETH. Go away. Shoo, go on.

(She stares. The **WHITE STAG** *crosses his arms and begins tapping a hoof. She pours a shot and knocks it back. Then sets the bottle and glass down again.)*

This is 70 Proof alcohol. It contains over 56 herbs, roots and spices and is best served 1° above freezing. They recommend that, the company. I recommend it, too. But it's an official recommendation.

WHITE STAG. You know it doesn't matter how much of that you drink, he's not calling you back.

ELIZABETH. And you know, I've seen people try to drink it warm. Can you [imagine?]

WHITE STAG. [Check your] phone. No missed calls.

ELIZABETH. It's best 1° above freezing.

WHITE STAG. No missed [calls.]

ELIZABETH. [A single] degree.

WHITE STAG. Have some more.

(**ELIZABETH** *pours and slams another shot. Things are getting a bit sloppier.*)

ELIZABETH. Just out of the freezer.

WHITE STAG. You can do better.

ELIZABETH. It tastes better.

WHITE STAG. Why would you want a guy who doesn't want you?

ELIZABETH. What kind of fucked up big-antlered question is that?

WHITE STAG. Okay, look, you can call him again and leave a message again and ask him to call you again and you'll just end up getting drunk again with me again like this [again and again.]

ELIZABETH. [Just shut the] fuck up, shut-up, you're not even real!

WHITE STAG. Um…I'm right here.

ELIZABETH. I said shoo, I shoo'd you away. Shoo, shoo.

WHITE STAG. Uh huh.

ELIZABETH. I will go and get a gun. I'm drunk.

WHITE STAG. And lonely.

ELIZABETH. I'm drunk.

WHITE STAG. And heartbroken.

ELIZABETH. I'm drunk!

WHITE STAG. You're drunk.

ELIZABETH. That's what I said!

(*An eerie green light reminiscent of the glass of a Jägermeister bottle illuminates the* **WHITE STAG** *as he recites the slogan. It fades as she overtakes him in volume.*)

WHITE STAG. "Das ist des Jägers [Ehrenschild, dass er beschützt und hegt sein Wild, weidmännisch jagt, wie sich's gehört, den Schöpfer im Geschöpfe ehrt."]

ELIZABETH. (*Slamming her fingers into her ears and speaking over him...*) [No, no, no, no, I can't hear you and your freaky German slogan banging around in my brain because it's the only thing I have to read because the bottle is the only thing in my fridge] and I don't want to go out and get anything else because I don't want to go out at all because he's out there somewhere and I don't want to see him even though I only want to see him, fuck, and your god damn slogan, which I don't really like, I only said that I like it, your bullshit slogan about good sportsmanship in hunting is the last fucking thing, the absolute last thing I need to be juxtaposing against my dating life!

(*She is breathing heavy, eyes closed tight, fingers still in her ears. The* WHITE STAG *just looks at her. After a moment she lowers her hands and catches her breath. Her eyes still closed.*)

WHITE STAG. It's not easy to find the right guy.

(*She opens her eyes and looks at him.*)

ELIZABETH. You're so...you're so understanding.

WHITE STAG. But, um, I'm not the right guy either.

ELIZABETH. Clearly.

WHITE STAG. I mean, you're attractive and all.

ELIZABETH. 1° above freezing.

(*The* WHITE STAG *crosses to* ELIZABETH *and gives her a hug. They break apart eventually.*)

WHITE STAG. Just the 1°. It's better cold.

ELIZABETH. It's better cold.

WHITE STAG. That's what I said.

ELIZABETH. This is hard.

WHITE STAG. I know.

ELIZABETH. Hunting's hard.

WHITE STAG. Hunting's hard on everyone.

ELIZABETH. Not like this though.

WHITE STAG. Just like this.

ELIZABETH. Really?

(*The* **WHITE STAG** *glows a bit brighter.*)

WHITE STAG. Really.

(*pause*)

ELIZABETH. I am so drunk.

WHITE STAG. You said that.

ELIZABETH. Well I am, so there.

WHITE STAG. But...you feel a little better?

ELIZABETH. A little.

WHITE STAG. Do you want me to say the German thing again?

ELIZABETH. No.

WHITE STAG. Okay.

(**ELIZABETH** *grabs the bottle and pours another shot.*)

It tastes like black licorice at first.

ELIZABETH. But only at first. Then it doesn't taste like anything.

(*She does the shot.*)

And then [you're here.]

WHITE STAG. [And then] I'm here.

ELIZABETH. And then [you're here.]

WHITE STAG. [And then] I'm here.

ELIZABETH. And then [you're here.]

WHITE STAG. [And then] I'm here.

ELIZABETH. And then [you're here.]

WHITE STAG. [And then] I'm here.

ELIZABETH. Like this.

(*The* **WHITE STAG** *pours a shot.*)

WHITE STAG. But then you stop and start over and it tastes like black licorice again.

ELIZABETH. That's...true.

WHITE STAG. It sounds like I'm advocating drinking, which I am, but you get that I'm actually talking about your love life?

ELIZABETH. Way to really lay it out there you stupid stag.

WHITE STAG. Well, you're drunk. I just want to be sure.

ELIZABETH. Whatever happened to subtlety?

WHITE STAG. You drank it.

ELIZABETH. Ugh, I'm gonna' be so hungover.

(The **WHITE STAG** *toasts* **ELIZABETH** *and knocks back the shot.)*

WHITE STAG. No question about it.

End

lucky

LIST OF PLAYERS

"PONY" SMITH: a young man, curious about the world, kept underground as a pet for a decade so his eyesight maybe isn't the best, also he has a collar

WHISKEY BARREL: a man, a Leprechaun, a big talker with big plans, bossy, prone to unexpected verbally abusive rants and dementia due to years of intense alcoholism

BICYCLE BELL: a woman, a Faerie, lithe, hard-edged in serious high heels, fitted skirt & blouse, and glasses, a severe and ill-humored minor functionary

NOTES

[ ] in the script indicate overlapping dialogue.

Whiskey Barrel's speech lives as a hodgepodge of Irish slang and contracted, drunken slur. Slap an Irish accent on it and have fun.

(**PONY** *is sitting with his legs crossed on the floor. The light is low. His hair is a mess and his clothes are several sizes too small. It's the clothing of a young boy and he's been wearing it way too long. He also wears a nice red dog collar. He is building a little castle out of discarded, dirty cola cans.*)

(**WHISKEY BARREL** *enters in a little green hat and brand new suspenders. He actually just stumbles in. He has a small canvas pouch in one hand and a bottle of whiskey in the other. He is clearly intoxicated as he knocks over the cola can castle.*)

PONY. Hey! I worked hard on that. Jeez.

WHISKEY BARREL. Aye now, young Pony. C'mere now, do you like my new suspenders?

PONY. I can't tell. They look like the old ones.

WHISKEY BARREL. They're plainly brand new and I'm quite proud of them!! Now you've been down here too long, lad. Your eyes have rotted right away from the darkness.

PONY. Huh. Um, I was just a little boy when I climbed into this storm drain to grab a shiny coin. Years and years without any sunshine is bound to mess up anyone's eyes, right?

WHISKEY BARREL. Well now that was my shiny coin you were aimin' for and now you're my loyal pet, aren't ya? Got you a nice collar and everything. Now c'mere then, why are you all out of sorts and bringin' up ancient history?

PONY. I don't like when you leave me down here alone. Where have you been?

WHISKEY BARREL. I ran an errand, didn't I? And you weren't alone.

PONY. Totally alone. In a storm drain. All of the other Leprechauns are gone. Remember? No? They packed up and left us here after you declined treatment at the intervention.

WHISKEY BARREL. I don't have a drinkin problem!!

(pause)

And I wasn't talkin about those other bollocksy Leprechauns. I was talking about our pigeon. Remind me now, what did we name him?

PONY. Bottle Cap.

WHISKEY BARREL. Bottle Cap! An excellent name! What about Bottle Cap?

PONY. He took my peanut butter and jelly sandwich, flew up into the corner over there, and never came back out. I can hear him cooing sometimes, but he won't come out.

WHISKEY BARREL. Well he's in a fowl mood, too. A "fowl" mood, ya know? I guess I'm the only one in a happy way today because I snuck into the Faerie camp with all their fancy Faerie security and stole their precious Faerie dust.

(He shows off the canvas pouch.)

And then I bought some whiskey. Because I deserved it, you understand.

(He drinks directly from the whiskey bottle.)

PONY. What kind did you get?

WHISKEY BARREL. You're sweet to ask, young Pony. What kind do you think?

PONY. I can smell it from here. Wait, don't tell me. I think it's a Dungourney 1964. No. No! Willie Napier 1945. You don't have to tell me, I'm right.

WHISKEY BARREL. That you are! I've trained you well! You do me proud, young Pony. There's not a Leprechaun with pockets full of gold anywhere that has an Irish Water Spaniel with a better nose.

PONY. I'm not an Irish Water Spaniel. And I don't like whiskey.

WHISKEY BARREL. Bollocks. Sometimes you say the oddest things.

*(They are interrupted as **BICYCLE BELL** enters. She's typing on her smart phone and doesn't look up. She's all business except for a small pair of wings.)*

BICYCLE BELL. This place is so fucking lame. How're you supposed to get reception down in a sewer? Does this even qualify as a sewer? I'm totally expensing these shoes; I don't give a fuck.

WHISKEY BARREL. Aye, would ya' look at that? It's a Faerie.

PONY. Where?! I can't see her? Is she talking to us?

WHISKEY BARREL. Hey there you wee Faerie lass, what're ya doin' down in our thrivin' Leprechaun colony.

PONY. Is she pretty?

BICYCLE BELL. Excuse me, are you a Leprechaun?

PONY. Tell me if she's pretty.

WHISKEY BARREL. Well now there has never been a greater Leprechaun than the one that stands before ya now and that's the truth.

*(**BICYCLE BELL** looks up from her phone.)*

BICYCLE BELL. I don't speak…whatever you're speaking. Are. You. A. Leprechaun?

WHISKEY BARREL. How about that now? She says she doesn't understand? I'm not speaking anything out of the ordinary. Comes [into my…]

BICYCLE BELL. [Okay. Okay.] Is *he* a Leprechaun?

PONY. Yes.

BICYCLE BELL. That was *so* easy, wasn't that *so* easy? And who are you?

PONY. Pony. I think that's my name. I'm a boy. Was a boy, now I'm a young man.

WHISKEY BARREL. Now don't listen to that eejit; he's an Irish Water Spaniel, loyal and true.

BICYCLE BELL. You're pretty clearly a human.

WHISKEY BARREL. He's an Irish. Water. [Spaniel.]

BICYCLE BELL. [What'd] they do, shrink you?

PONY. Yes.

BICYCLE BELL. And keep you as a pet?

PONY. Yes.

BICYCLE BELL. Well that's an unfortunate story. And you should get some new clothes. Look, I'm here on behalf of Tinker Bell and her entire Faerie cadre so we can enter into negotiations to get her stolen Faerie dust back. Can we just do that?

WHISKEY BARREL. Aye, well, Ms. Tinker Bell can't be bothered to come 'round here herself?

PONY. I don't...what?

PONY. He was wryly noting that Tinker Bell didn't come down here herself.

BICYCLE BELL. Of course she didn't. Of. Course. She. Didn't. Did you get that? Did he get that? She's *way* too famous to go out in public now and I can't imagine anyone would willingly climb down into this sewer. Unless they were tricked. Or had to. Oh, but it's lovely. Or something. I'm Bicycle Bell, I'm sort of like a "bag man." I get things done.

(**WHISKEY BARREL** *laughs.*)

WHISKEY BARREL. Bicycle Bell?

BICYCLE BELL. I just can't. It's really like he's talking with a mouth full of rocks.

PONY. He thinks your name is funny.

BICYCLE BELL. Excuse me! Clearly you're not in the know about *anything* except whatever's in that fucking bottle, so let me break it down for you: the more authority you have as a Faerie, the smaller and lovelier your name gets. *Nothing* could be tinier and cuter than a tinker bell because she's at the very top. A bicycle bell is pretty small and relatively adorable, so clearly I've got moxie. It's not like my name is gong or something. If my name was gong then *maybe* he could laugh. Tell him that. *Tell him.*

PONY. He heard you. He speaks English.

(She looks dubious.)

BICYCLE BELL. Hmmm. So you're Pony. And I'm Bicycle Bell, which to reiterate is totally adorable. And you are?

WHISKEY BARREL. Whiskey Barrel.

PONY. Whiskey Barrel the Leprechaun.

BICYCLE BELL. Your name is Whiskey Barrel?

WHISKEY BARREL. Aye, Whiskey Barrel. It's a [pleasure to…]

BICYCLE BELL. [Just to be] *ultra* fucking clear, your name is Whiskey Barrel and you were laughing at *my* name?

WHISKEY BARREL. Now go on outta' that, I don't have your Faerie dust and you're wastin' your time down here. Good luck!

*(**BICYCLE BELL** sighs and shakes her head. She looks at **PONY**.)*

PONY. He says he doesn't have your Faerie dust.

BICYCLE BELL. It's in his hand.

WHISKEY BARREL. No, now, this is Irish whiskey. It's, uh, the brand is, uh…

PONY. Willie Napier 1945.

WHISKEY BARREL. Aye, that's what it is! And never has [there been…]

BICYCLE BELL. [Are you fucking] kidding me? It's in his *other* hand.

WHISKEY BARREL. Begorrah! Look at that?! A bag of Faerie dust!

BICYCLE BELL. And we need it back. *Please.* You're probably too drunk to realize this, but there's a nasty fucking plague on humanity happening up there.

PONY. A plague?!

BICYCLE BELL. Yes. On humanity. Some kind of alien plague.

PONY. Aliens?!

BICYCLE BELL. Yes. Stop shouting. An alien plague on humanity and our Faerie dust is the only cure. Or else they'll all die. So your timing is pretty poor.

PONY. Oh no.

(**PONY** *starts to cry.*)

BICYCLE BELL. Oh wait, was that insensitive? I keep thinking of you as a *Spaniel* and not a young man, not a person; it's mostly because I'm not really paying attention. Forget I said "plague." It's pretty bad, but plague is a scary word. And I'm sure whoever you know is fine. Or something. Anyway, let's get this negotiation underway.

PONY. Give her the bag!!

WHISKEY BARREL. Quiet ya wee Spaniel! It's mine now and I mean to keep [hold of it.]

PONY. [I don't remember] anyone from up there but I don't want them to die!

BICYCLE BELL. Okay, I'm starting to get a hold on this. I think. If I understand you correctly then you don't plan on giving back the Faerie dust?

WHISKEY BARREL. I'm not that hard to understand. And not for this entire colony.

BICYCLE BELL. This entire colony *appears* to be one drunken Leprechaun that I can smell from here and a boy with a dog collar in a sewer drain.

WHISKEY BARREL. We also have a pigeon named Bottle Cap!

BICYCLE BELL. Strange young dog man, do you want all of humanity to die?

PONY. No! No!

BICYCLE BELL. Well then could *you* talk to him?

PONY. Whiskey Barrel, I've been a good dog, haven't I?

WHISKEY BARREL. Aye.

PONY. And I've never tried to run away, have I?

WHISKEY BARREL. That's true.

PONY. And I've never asked for anything.

WHISKEY BARREL. Most Spaniels wouldn't offer up such a fluffy preamble about their relationship to their owner, but you've never asked for a thing.

PONY. I'm only asking this one thing: please don't let all of humanity die from an alien plague just to spite the Faeries. When you sober up, you'll regret it.

WHISKEY BARREL. Aye, well now, I'm never goin' to sober up, so that's a bit of a faulty argument. And I'm not keepin' this sack out of spite. I find the Faerie dust to be soothin' in my bath water. It makes the water bubble.

BICYCLE BELL. False.

PONY. You've never taken a bath in all the years I've been here!

WHISKEY BARREL. Then I imagine it would be soothing in my bath water.

PONY. *Still* false.

WHISKEY BARREL. And don't you make it sound like I'm some dirty little man; I'm magical and I don't need to bathe.

BICYCLE BELL. *So false.*

PONY. You can't let all the people die!

WHISKEY BARREL. Now don't you go tellin' me what I can [and can't do!]

PONY. [If all the people] die then there won't be anyone left to make whiskey!

(*Pause.* **WHISKEY BARREL** *looks terrified. But then he starts laughing.*)

WHISKEY BARREL. You had me worried for a minute, didn't ya? But there's plenty of whiskey in the world. And if all those people go away, well, that'll be all the more for me.

BICYCLE BELL. You are ridiculous; just give me the fucking Faerie dust.

WHISKEY BARREL. Quiet you! You're rude and getting less pretty by the moment. You Faerie folk don't have anything I need because I went on and took the only thing I wanted from ya. So I'm thinkin' there won't be any "negotiation."

BICYCLE BELL. Are you *really* going to make me get rough and rattle around your dementia addled brain in your alcohol soaked skull?

WHISKEY BARREL. I'm a lot more agile than you'd imagine.

(He takes a huge swig of whiskey.)

BICYCLE BELL. All right, *you know what?*

(She kicks off her heels, adjusts her skirt, and sets her smart phone down. She then rushes **WHISKEY BARREL** *and knocks him to the ground. They struggle over the bag. He's bigger, but drunk, so it's a real battle. They scrap and claw, tugging on the canvas bag.* **PONY** *gets out of the way and stares in shock.)*

WHISKEY BARREL. Let go! I stole it [fair and square.]

BICYCLE BELL. [Let go of it] you crazy [fucking Leprechaun.]

WHISKEY BARREL. [How is such a] wee lass [so strong?]

BICYCLE BELL. [I will claw your] fucking face off!

(Suddenly the bag rips open and the Faerie dust glitter flies everywhere. Everywhere. It covers everything. It covers all three of them. There's so much Faerie dust glitter that no one will ever clean it up. Ever. The explosion of glitter from the bag is accompanied by a deafening cacophony of sparkling bells and a blast of illumination as the previously dim lights flare up and flood the stage, briefly bathing everything in moving colors and brilliant light. Just as quickly the moment ends. **PONY** *sits, mouth agape, taking in the moment.* **BICYCLE BELL** *and* **WHISKEY BARREL** *are out of breath and clearly disappointed.)*

PONY. *(quietly...)* That was the most beautiful thing I've ever seen.

(Pause. **BICYCLE BELL** *gets up, grabs her shoes, and picks up her phone.)*

WHISKEY BARREL. Now I'll never have my bubble bath.

BICYCLE BELL. I fucking *hate* you. And just look at these shoes. *Ruined.* How am I going to explain this? I'm so going to be downgraded to at least a hand bell.

PONY. But what about all of the people?!

BICYCLE BELL. I guess they'll just have to do their fucking best. Maybe they'll get lucky.

(She exits. **WHISKEY BARREL** *toasts after her with the bottle and drinks.)*

End of Play

bedtime

LIST OF PLAYERS

VIOLET: a young woman, effortlessly sexy and oddly confident, the probable heroine in the end

JULIE: a young woman, naïve but observant, a good friend who is really put to the test

BAG MAN: a man, hulking, looming, dirty, and probably horribly disfigured underneath the bag he wears on his head, a serious stalker

NOTES

[ ] in the script indicate overlapping dialogue.

(Lights up on an empty room. Well, mostly empty except for a bare mattress sitting on the floor. JULIE wears an oversized nightshirt and carries her folded clothes and an overnight kit. VIOLET leads her into the room. She is wearing a nightgown and has a towel wrapped around something.)

JULIE. Is this where I'm sleeping?

VIOLET. *(laughing)* Oh no, of course not. Julie, I wouldn't make you sleep in here.

JULIE. Where is everything?

VIOLET. I just didn't want to get anything else messy.

JULIE. Messy?

VIOLET. Oh, you know.

JULIE. What?

VIOLET. I set up the fold out couch for you while you were getting changed. It's just out in the den and it's very comfortable. Or I think so anyway. No one's ever complained about it at least.

JULIE. Oh, good.

VIOLET. And there are extra blankets in the hall closet if you need them. Just down there.

JULIE. Great.

VIOLET. Mm hm.

JULIE. So then, okay. I think I'll call it a night.

VIOLET. Of course. Just...I'm going to need you to stay in here. Not all night, like I said, I made up the couch. But just until it's fully dark outside.

JULIE. Violet, what's going on?

VIOLET. I think it's so great of you to agree to crash here tonight. Really. I have no idea what I would have done in this house all by myself after they found Billy's body all mangled up like that in the back yard.

JULIE. It's terrible.

VIOLET. There were pieces missing. Did I tell you?

JULIE. No.

VIOLET. Little pieces of Billy. And his face had been entirely smashed in from some [kind of...]

JULIE. [Oh my] god!

VIOLET. Even though we'd only been on three dates, it was heartbreaking. And I started laughing. Did I tell you? I was going to scream, but it came out as this uncontrollable laughter and I started kicking him to wake him up, it was just insane that he could ever wake up after being so [thoroughly...]

JULIE. [Please, please] don't talk about it.

VIOLET. Sorry.

(awkward pause)

JULIE. No, it's...I just get uncomfortable with. I mean...unless you need to talk about it? I want to be here for you.

VIOLET. That's because you're my best friend and the one person I can count on. But I don't want to talk about it. And I don't want to deprive you of your sleep. So I just need you to stay in here for a little bit longer and then we can both go to bed.

(She unwraps an unusually large pair of shearing scissors.)

JULIE. Whoa.

VIOLET. I know, right? They're kind of threatening, aren't they?

JULIE. What are you doing with a huge pair of scissors?

VIOLET. Shears, actually.

JULIE. What are you doing with them?

(She stabs the air a few times. JULIE slowly backs away from her.)

VIOLET. I'm sort of, sort of psyching myself up.

JULIE. What did you mean by messy, Violet?

VIOLET. Have you ever seen the movie *Friday the 13th?*

JULIE. No.

VIOLET. *Texas Chainsaw Massacre?*

JULIE. No.

VIOLET. Really? What about *Halloween?* Everyone's seen *Halloween.*

JULIE. I don't like those kinds of movies.

VIOLET. That's fascinating, all horror movies or just Slasher films? You know what? It doesn't matter. It's just, and I'm not criticizing you or anything, but the basic premise of all this would be so much easier if you had seen at least one Slasher flick.

JULIE. Okay, you're starting to freak me out.

VIOLET. Oh, no. That's not what I'm trying to do. All right, honestly? Honestly, I've kept a huge secret from you, Julie.

JULIE. Oh my god, you killed Billy?

VIOLET. No! No, what's wrong with you? I would never.

JULIE. What am I supposed to think? You stripped this room bare and you're waving around a giant pair of scissors and, I don't know, you're acting bizarre.

VIOLET. Julie, you're my best friend. I think I've said that at least twice tonight now. Once or twice. Anyway, I could never hurt you.

JULIE. Okay.

VIOLET. And if you'd stop interrupting me then I could explain.

(JULIE *starts to speak.* VIOLET *puts her hands on her hips.* JULIE *stops.*)

Okay. Basically, and this is the quick version, there's this mysterious, insane man who's been stalking me for years. I just call him the "bag man" because he wears a bag on his head. I don't know much about him because he never speaks, he just does this breathing thing, this loud breathing thing. But I assume he's all disfigured under that bag because that's kind of par for the course with these things. Beyond that, I don't have much to go on. Also, and don't freak out or get upset with me, but he sort of kills everyone who gets close to me.

JULIE. Oh my god.

VIOLET. I know, right? Blah, blah, blah, I don't like to talk about it because I just sound so whiney. And like a total victim, it's so pathetic. Anyway, it's manageable because he only comes at night and only when other people are in the house. That's the real reason that I never host game night, even though I know how much it annoys you. But I had to be careful, even though it hadn't happened in years. And I begged Billy to go home, but he thought after the third date was a good time to be romantic or whatever. So I guess he tried to sneak in my bedroom window. You know, romance? And then the "bag man" pulled him back outside, threw him off the ladder and killed him.

JULIE. Oh my god!

VIOLET. Exactly. So clearly he's still around and killing people. But, and this is a good thing, Julie, after four nervous breakdowns and I don't know how many funerals, it's finally time for me to fight back. I mean, I really liked Billy, ya' know? It's just too much.

(pause)

JULIE. That can't be true.

VIOLET. I hate to say this, Julie. But if you had a working knowledge of the genre this would all seem a lot more plausible, honestly.

JULIE. That's the worst thing I've ever heard.

VIOLET. Isn't it?

JULIE. That's, Violet, that's the worst thing I've ever heard.

VIOLET. I believe you. Now focus, okay? Since you're staying in the house, and you count as someone close to me, I just need us to wait in this room in case things get messy.

JULIE. So let me just…

(She looks around and then pointedly drops all of her belongings.)

JULIE. I'm bait?

VIOLET. In a manner of speaking, but don't think of it like that. Just stay out of the way when he gets here.

JULIE. I'm bait for a psycho killer!!?

VIOLET. You said if there was anything you could do. You said that.

JULIE. To comfort you!

VIOLET. This is absolutely comforting.

JULIE. Violet! What if you can't kill him? Is he going to kill me too?

VIOLET. Let's say, "no."

JULIE. We are fully going to die.

VIOLET. Now look, we have to be optimistic, Julie.

VIOLET. Optimistic!? I didn't, this is insane.

VIOLET. Yes.

JULIE. Are you insane?

VIOLET. Maybe.

JULIE. I think you're insane.

VIOLET. I mean, I've been through a lot, Julie.

JULIE. That's…fair.

VIOLET. Thank you.

JULIE. But I don't want to die.

VIOLET. Nobody wants to die.

JULIE. I'm leaving right now.

VIOLET. Julie, please.

JULIE. Get out of my way.

VIOLET. Please. All you have to do is stand there. Just stand there. If it looks like I'm not going to, if it looks bad then run. He won't chase you if I'm here. I don't think.

(She begins to tear up but fights it.)

You have to help me. I don't know what else to do, but whatever happens tonight, I'm not going to be afraid anymore. I can't keep living in fear. Alone. And afraid.

JULIE. Violet, I don't…

>   *(pause)*

>   I just have to stand here.

>   *(**VIOLET** gives **JULIE** a huge hug.)*

VIOLET. Thank you!

JULIE. Don't cut me with those things.

>   *(**VIOLET** pulls away.)*

>   It's dark out. So…what now?

>   *(A huge man in a long-sleeved plaid shirt, jeans and heavy boots lumbers into the light. He is breathing heavy, chest and shoulders visibly rising and falling. He wears a horrifying, featureless burlap sack on his head with eyeholes cut out. He carries a huge lug wrench in one hand. **JULIE** gasps in shock and stumbles backward onto the mattress. She looks to **VIOLET** in horror. **VIOLET** stares at the man and slowly holds out the immense scissors aggressively.)*

VIOLET. And here we go.

End

a lovely violent ghost
haiku with gun

LIST OF PLAYERS

BOY: a teenage boy, a bit of a hooligan, a bit of a cocky punk in the way that teenage boys can be before they grow up

GIRL: a teenage girl, trendy but dark, going through the normal angst of adolescence but not in the "normal" way

NOTES

[ ] in the script indicate overlapping dialogue.

Girls' haikus probably have a bit of a creepy, "sing songy" quality to them as she strings them together.

(A GIRL sits in an empty alley at night. Quiet. A BOY wanders up with a smile. An unseen street lamp flickers.)

BOY. Here you are.

GIRL. It's late and it's dark,

Dark street, dark night, buzzing light

My eyes are swimmy

(She lights the cigarette.)

BOY. They should fix that fucking light, huh?

GIRL. I like when it flashes.

BOY. It's fucked.

GIRL. Ugh, I can't even taste this, why can't I taste this?

(She puts out the cigarette. He leans in and kisses her. She kisses him and then looks down, pulling her face away. She laughs. He smiles.)

BOY. What's so funny?

GIRL. You're lips are warm.

BOY. And you're cold to the touch; you should have a jacket.

GIRL. I'm…fine.

BOY. Why are you even out here? I've been looking for you and, and I've got something to say.

(Pause. He waits. She doesn't look up.)

But if you're in a bad mood…?

GIRL. I'm not. I'm just, I'm in a weird mood. No, it's stupid. I'm glad you're here.

BOY. What's wrong.

GIRL. I didn't say anything's wrong.

BOY. Then what's "weird?"

GIRL. You know I got in a fight after school with that new girl, Beatrix Shimizu?

67

BOY. That's her name? Huh. Sure, the police stopped us outside the arcade. They were looking for you. So, uh, you must have really knocked her out?

GIRL. I'm good in a fight.

BOY. Oh, absolutely.

GIRL. She was being so mean; saying these nasty things, pony tails swinging.

BOY. Those cops asked us all these questions. Stone-faced. We told them to fuck off. Girl fight! Fuck off! You should have seen; they were so serious.

GIRL. Beatrix Shimizu said you kissed her. I didn't believe her.

BOY. Well, I mean...I did.

GIRL. Oh. Okay. Oh. I shouldn't have called her a liar then.

BOY. She, like, dared me. In front of people. It didn't mean anything. She's trashy anyway. And her name is stupid.

GIRL. She's not trashy though. She's pretty, isn't she? Prettier than me. She has bright eyes. And her hair is so shiny; it doesn't get all crazy like mine.

BOY. I mean she is pretty, okay, [but you're...]

GIRL. [Stinging in] my ears
You like her better, my heart
So fast, stop, so fast

BOY. I don't like her better. And why are you talking like that?

GIRL. Haiku. We're studying it in class. I'm practicing.

BOY. It reminds of that sign by your house: "Warning: moving gate can cause serious injury or death." With the stick figure getting crushed. "Argh."

(He pantomimes being crushed to death by a moving gate.)

GIRL. That's not right. That's not the right number [of words...]

BOY. [It just] reminds me of the sign. Anyway, I like you best, okay? I wanted to find you because I've been meaning [to say…]

GIRL. [I shot] her. I shot Beatrix Shimizu. She was laughing at me with her perfect hair and kissing mouth and tongue-twister name and I shot her.

BOY. You did not.

GIRL. I did.

BOY. They didn't say that, the police, just that you hurt [her…]

GIRL. [Really,] she just fell over. And then I shot a man on the street tonight.

BOY. Okay, now I know you're fucking with me.

GIRL. It was easier the second time.

BOY. Shut-up.

GIRL. He looked really calm even though his life was must have been very difficult and then bumped me, on the train, talking so loudly on his cell phone, yelling about some meeting he missed, maybe an accident, but he didn't apologize. He sneered. He sneered at me. So I followed [him when…]

BOY. [And so] you shot him? I don't believe you. You didn't shoot anybody.

GIRL. Maybe there was no
Shooting in the streets tonight
Hard to remember

BOY. I wish you'd stop that; it's creepy.

GIRL. Have you kissed a lot of other girls?

BOY. Look, it doesn't even, just…I love you, okay?

GIRL. Oh. Wow. I wish you'd…you can't.

BOY. I do. I came to find you because I wanted to tell you. And now I did.

GIRL. Oh.

BOY. You should be happy or something. I've been waiting to tell you. Ever since we stood in the alley behind that jazz club and you let me dance with you. It was so dark, but I could feel your breath and I've never heard music like that. My heart was beating. And you were so beautiful and I just, well, I mean I've never been in love before so I don't know how I'm supposed to, but this is totally love. It has to be.

GIRL. After I shot those other people I shot myself.

BOY. Now you're just being crazy, what is wrong with you. I'm telling you I love you. That's, like, a big fucking deal. Stop whatever this [is and...]

GIRL. [Look at] me, look right here.

(She pulls back her hair, it is hidden from sight, but he can see it and his eyes go wide.)

BOY. Oh my god, fuck, what [did you...]

GIRL. [I thought] I would die. But I didn't want to be lonely. So I'm still here.

BOY. Hoy fuck, you shot yourself in [the head?]

GIRL. [Say it again,] okay?

BOY. What?

GIRL. Say that you love me.

BOY. You need to go to the hospital!

GIRL. Please.

BOY. "All those people." That's what you, how many people did [you shoot?]

GIRL. [A lot. Please.]

BOY. A lot?!

GIRL. Please say it for me.

(She pulls a gun out of her bag.)

BOY. What are you, okay, [okay, okay...]

GIRL. [I didn't want] to be alone, I wanted to see you. I thought that would make me less lonely.

BOY. Please don't shoot me.

GIRL. Say it!

BOY. I love you. I do!

(She shoots him. His body spins to the ground.)

GIRL. All the girls like you,
But you like me best of all,
So I should feel better

(Pause. She counts syllables then laughs.)

No, that one wasn't right. And I don't, it's not your fault, but I don't feel less lonely. I thought…Ugh, I'm just gonna' keep shooting people, okay? Tell me if you think that's a bad idea.

(pause)

I'll wait.

End

wallpaper

LIST OF PLAYERS

LINDSAY: a woman, paranoid and charming, nervous but likeable, probably a psychopath but able to make her way through the world so far

WOMAN: a trendy woman who steps out of the group of people to become Lindsay's next object of obsession

NOTES

[ ] in the script indicate overlapping dialogue.

The group of bystanders called for should be as large as possible: stage hands, actors from other plays, people off the street with a passion for theatre, whatever works.

*(Lights rise to reveal **PEOPLE** in a tight group standing on stage. They are all looking up, off into the distance at the same something.)*

*(**LINDSAY** enters, pushing past the group. She is disheveled in a long coat, but trying to look good. Trying.)*

LINDSAY. Too many people, right. Even at night, this late, it's so busy, feels like everyone is just flying right by, ya' know? Not just tonight, always. It's so easy if you stop and think for a second to just get shoved to the side, or trampled even. That's just so, and I, I try not to let it get to me, but the dark doesn't help, the streetlights so harsh. I feel like I'm on a television show and I'm the only one who knows it. Or the worst is on the train. Or I guess a bus or any kind of place like that? Oh! An elevator! But I don't ride in those, small spaces, so for me really it's the train. I wish I could explain how it gets under my skin and just, okay, all right, I have this dream all the time. I think this is a solid example to maybe explain how it feels. I have this dream, it just kinda' comes over me. So in this dream, it's late at night and I'm on the train. And it's packed, I mean stuffed to bursting. Like if the doors open, people just spill out on their backs and then we keep moving right along. And I'm in the middle. And there are television screens all along the inside of the train car and they're all showing cooking shows, but in French. And there's a frog on the shoulder of the guy right in front of me. Like a little tree frog? And he's got his back to me, the man and the little frog on his shoulder, but we're squeezed so tight that I'm just very close and I'm sure the little tree frog can feel my breath on his back. Which must be so uncomfortable, but what can I do?

*(The **PEOPLE** all take a deep breathe in unison.)*

LINDSAY. *(cont.)* Right before my stop the little frog turns
around on the guys shoulder and looks at me, right in
my eyes, which is very awkward. But he smiles a little
frog smile with his little big eyes and says, "Crowded
today, huh?" and I say, "Yes." And he says, "I hate this
television show because I don't speak French." And
I say, "Me either…" and we laugh a bit. And he says,
"Do you happen to have any peanut butter?" And I say,
"Not with me, but I have some at home." And he says,
"Well listen, I am craving peanut butter right now and
it's so crowded, could I trouble you for a spoonful?"
And I say, "Well, that sounds okay I guess. I certainly
have it to spare." And he says, "Excellent." And the
train jerks to a stop, we spill out and he follows me
home. Only I have to walk very slowly because he's a
very small frog. And I have to be careful because it's
dark and I would feel really terrible if I stepped on
him. Let me tell you, it takes him forever to get up
the stairs to my place. But it seems impolite to offer to
help. I mean he made it from whatever jungle all the
way to my steps on his own.

Anyway, we get inside and I'm a bit embarrassed because
I've left the television on it's quite loud. In French. I
switch it off as discretely as you can do something like
that and I go the cabinet. I open it up and there are
thousands of jars of peanut butter. Thousands. All different brands, so many labels and colors and choices.
And as I'm trying to figure out which peanut butter is
best for tree frogs, which is nerve racking because he's
right there looking around my place, he says, "This is
very unusual wallpaper." And when I turn to look, I
see on my wall this image of my 10th grade biology lab
with a partially dissected frog, cut half-open with pins
and clamps and refrigerated blood everywhere, all on
my wall. That image over and over and over again. The
tree frog turns to look at me and, obviously, he's not
at all pleased. I start to apologize when suddenly he
jumps onto the counter, stabs me in the neck with a

kitchen knife, stabs me multiple times with blood just gushing out and I have to hold my hands like this to try and stop it. And he runs off with a bunch of peanut butter while I lay on the floor bleeding to death.

(The **PEOPLE** *all look at their wrists, even though they don't have watches, and then return to staring up. The sounds of clocks ticking, different wristwatches.)*

LINDSAY. *(cont.)* So you see why I hate people then? I mean trains, you see why I hate trains then? And television. But that was about trains. I'm sorry, maybe not. It's so hard to focus with all of these people around. I try to put things together in my head when I'm walking down the street or at the store, anywhere, but if I try too hard, it's like there are hundreds of birds right above my head just making the most awful…

(The **PEOPLE** *begin to loudly make various bird sounds while remaining motionless.* **LINDSAY** *looks at them crossly and waits for them to stop. She her ears and clearly annoyed and struggling. The* **PEOPLE** *stop.* **LINDSAY** *cautiously lowers her hands…)*

Finally. I didn't think that would ever stop. You could hear that, right? I hope you could hear that, I hope it wasn't just me. People can be so, just, ugh. But you try, ya' know, try to learn to still get through. Or at least just stay away from people. I just stay away from people. But that gets lonely but I've adapted, when I really need someone to notice me. When I need someone to do something nice or say something nice, I'll just invent an imaginary friend. Not like the frog, the frog was real. Dream real. Anyway, I've been doing that since I was little, making up friends. And they say you grow out of it, but that's only because you make real friends. If you don't do that, then you never lose the ability to make really great imaginary ones. Bet you didn't know that, huh? The only problem with imaginary friends though is that they have a definite shelf life. Does that make sense? They are good for a while, but they start to get unruly and mean after a time and that's when they have to go. It's sad, but it's a simple fact. I remember Sally, my very first imaginary friend when I was little. She was wonderful, she would come around sometimes and play, she made up this story about how she lived down the block and it was so detailed. She was a great imaginary friend. And she was so nice. But after a while, Sally wanted to go do things with other kids and I didn't understand that at all. But she was adamant, so one day I choked the life out of her, which is the best way to deal with an imaginary friend. She kept crying and saying she wanted to go home and see her Mommy, but I wasn't fooled for a second. And then I hid her little imaginary body in the woods so that my parents wouldn't be cross. Her imaginary Mom came to ask my parents about it, but they didn't know anything.

(She smiles.)

LINDSAY. *(cont.)* I've had to do that a lot of times over the years. Kill them.

*(The **PEOPLE** begin loudly making the bird noises again, only briefly this time, and then stop.)*

I have a special place in the woods where they all go. It's a little bit of a drive now that I live in the city, but I don't mind it. It brings back such fond memories. And it's away from all of these noisy, busy people. And the fucking twenty-four hour a day talk-shows and trains and shopping networks and all of that where it's like I don't even exist here. I'm just a background. No one sees me. And it's lonely, even though I say I don't like people, so I watch a lot of television even though I hate it. Ugh, sometimes you just want someone to notice you.

*(The **PEOPLE** all take a loud step in unison. This startles **LINDSAY** and she drops her bag. It spills open.)*

Oh no! All my things…

*(A **WOMAN** suddenly breaks from her pose, stepping out of the group. She bends down to help **LINDSAY** collect the items...)*

WOMAN. Oh, I hate it when that happens.

LINDSAY. It's just a bit embarrassing is all; I'm sorry.

WOMAN. Happens to everyone though. Oh, look, this compact is adorable. Where did you get it? Did I see this in a commercial or something?

(They rise, having collected everything...)

It's too precious. And that bag. I can see we have similar tastes.

LINDSAY. You like it?

WOMAN. Absolutely. Look I was just going in here to grab a coffee. It's to late for coffee, but you want one? I have to know where you got that compact.

LINDSAY. That's so nice. That's just so nice, that's just what I needed to hear. Let's be friends.

*(The **PEOPLE** caw again in a flurry of bird sounds. Blackout.)*

End

when it happens
it will happen quietly

LIST OF PLAYERS

KITH: a woman, lithe, constantly moving loose hair out of her face that has slipped from her bun, coming into her own

KIN: a woman, perhaps a bit smaller, a bit weaker, but clearly the peace-maker in the family, Kith's little sister

NOTES

[ ] in the script indicate overlapping dialogue.

The entire play should have a hushed quality.

(**KITH** *and* **KIN** *sit at a small table quietly eating with spoons from a pair of bowls.*)

KIN. The soup is so warm.

KITH. It's not soup; it's stew. It's heartier, you know?

KIN. I can't believe Dad actually let you make something to eat. I feel like I haven't eaten in days now. And the way he guards the icebox.

KITH. Refrigerator.

KIN. Refrigerator. And the way he won't let [us have…]

KITH. [Selfish.]

KIN. He's doing what he thinks is [right, I guess.]

KITH. [Don't do that,] don't defend him. You're always doing that. You're filial devotion just wears on me, honestly. I mean look at us, we barely get anything. He's a monster.

KIN. Well, these are lean times.

KITH. "Lean times?" You're doing it again, right now. Making excuses. I swear. Just eat before it gets cold.

(*pause*)

KIN. What was, what was that noise in the kitchen?

KITH. Nothing.

KIN. It sounded like muffled [shouting…]

KITH. [Well, he tried] to stop me, of course.

KIN. Oh.

KITH. But now we have stew, so…enjoy it.

(**KIN** *gives her a look and then sets down the soup.*)

Fine. Fine, I killed him, all right? He wouldn't let me into the refrigerator so I killed Dad and then I butchered him and then I put him in the stew. Well, part of him anyway. With some carrots. And a bit of black pepper.

(Pause. **KIN** *looks at the bowl and then at her sister.* **KITH** *gives her a nod and a warm smile.* **KIN** *begins eating again.)*

KIN. It's delicious.

KITH. Thank you.

KIN. You're welcome.

KITH. And don't worry; now there's plenty.

(They continue quietly eating.)

End

very still & hard to see

a short play cycle

LIST OF PLAYERS

OBAKE: a "woman" but more of a secret thing, striking, poised, polite and not at all what she appears

 also **MUD WOMAN**, a ghost of love now made dirty and limp, but with a beautiful voice

BUCK: a man, an architect used to giving orders and practiced at masking a hidden hunger

 also **SHIKIGAMI 2** with glasses & pencil behind his ear

 also **CANARY,** a victim of physical abuse

ETHAN: a man, Betty's husband, handsome, but lots of sleepless nights and time to wander

 also **SAM**, a pretty amiable boyfriend right to the end

 also **GUEST**, very weary and ready for bed

BETTY: a woman with trouble sleeping and a need to clean

 also **KAMI 1**, quiet but full of anxiety and history

 also **VIOLET,** a potential love interest

EDITH: a woman, a nervous wife, still jovial in grappling with tragedy

 also **SHIKIGAMI 1,** upbeat with glasses and a giant book

 also **PUNCH**, demanding and oddly domestic

GINGER: a woman, caught between who she'd like to be and what she's actually done – and still does

 also **KIMBERLY,** a good girlfriend right to the end

 also, **SIMONE**, a romantic, entrenched pill head

FRANKLIN: a man, a bit sassy and very rule-oriented, unaware of his actions, or maybe aware – which would be worse

 also, **JASPER**, a bit of a third wheel in the wrong room

DAVID: a man, Simone's husband, no fan of attention, but patiently doing his best

 also **KAMI 2**, quiet but full of tension and history

NOTES

[ ] indicate overlapping dialogue

This cycle of seven short plays is divided into nine parts:

Obake and **bakemono** are a class of yōkai, preternatural creatures in Japanese folklore. Literally, the terms mean a thing that changes, referring to a state of transformation or shapeshifting. Often translated as ghost, the term primarily refers to living things or supernatural beings who have taken on a temporary transformation. A bakemono's true form may be an animal or inanimate object but it will usually disguises itself as a human or appear in some strange and terrifying form. **Whenever ensemble members are not in a main role, they are a part of the unseen mass behind the "Obake" character.**

Kami are manifestations of "spiritual essence," commonly translated as god or spirit. **When Kami 1 appears in ( ) after Jasper, it means she is whispering the lines as Jasper speaks them aloud.**

Shikigami are a kind of spirit, found in Japanese Mythology, summoned to serve a practitioner of onmyōdō, much like a western familiar. Shikigami cannot be seen by most people.

The setting of the play is a large circle inscribed in some way on a bare stage. This circle represents a variety of locales and objects throughout the plays. **It may be useful to use a larger circle with a smaller circle inscribed.** There is also a single chair.

Any additional props, set pieces or costumes should be present around the periphery of the stage, but not inside the circle. Each primary character's base costume need only be slightly altered by minor additions or subtractions to create the supporting roles.

prologue

(The ensemble is on stage milling about. Perhaps they are creating the circles that will demarcate the floor plan.)

*(The **OBAKE** sits in a chair, taking in the audience.)*

*(When everything is ready to begin, the **OBAKE** rises as the ensemble groups inside the circles. They look to her. She looks at them, smiles and then offers a nod.)*

(In unison, the ensemble inhales sharply and then exhales, collapsing into the circle, falling limp and lifeless onto the floor.)

*(The **OBAKE** takes in the scene, turns and then smiles to the audience as the lights crash to black.)*

End Scene

i. under ground

*(Deep in the ground. **BUCK** tries to stand in the circle
but can't. Eyes adjusting, he is dirty, bleeding and holds
a handkerchief to his head.)*

(Something moves outside of the circle.)

BUCK. Hello? Damn it, I can't…

(looking up)

Can you guys hear me?! Hello!? God damn it, how am
I [going to…?]

*(The **OBAKE** stands just out outside the light. She is
striking, lovely, dressed simply. The rest of the cast
pools behind her, a **MASS** of sounds and whispers that
underscore her voice, sometimes speaking along with her,
beneath her. As she moves around the circle, they move
behind her, a part of her – the unseen horror of her form.)*

OBAKE. [How is] your head?

BUCK. Fuck!

OBAKE. Such language. Tsk tsk. How is your head, does it
hurt?

BUCK. Where are you, I can't see you?

OBAKE. Hmm, that's for the best.

BUCK. Come out where I can see you.

OBAKE. Shhh, it's too dark. Now, what are you doing down
here?

BUCK. I fell down some, the construction site is up there,
my building, and I fell through a sinkhole or some
[kind of…]

OBAKE. [Ah, well,] this is where I live. I live down here.
Do you like it? I don't mind telling you, it's been such
a long time since anyone's visited. I'd offer you some
aspirin, but as you can see I live a very spare lifestyle.

BUCK. Are you going to come out where I can see you?

OBAKE. The cupboards are bare.

(She smiles. The **MASS** *snickers and quietly laughs behind her.)*

BUCK. Listen to me, I'm ultimately in charge of this build, I'm the boss, okay? My name is Buck Mason and I designed this fucking building. I'm in charge. So whoever you are, you shouldn't be down here and I will make [sure that...]

(Laughing. She steps into view, poised, well dressed, sharp and clean. Not at all what's expected.)

OBAKE. [You know,] I used to just love to sew, can you imagine? The motion of my hands, moving the thread, the specificity of it. Feeling the work in my fingers. But the low light down here is murder on my eyes.

BUCK. What is this?

OBAKE. Just a visit. I've been asleep for so long, but all of your banging around woke me up, Buck Mason. So now we're having a little visit.

BUCK. Or I hit my head harder than I thought.

OBAKE. Maybe. Maybe that's what this is. It's so dark after all. Eyes adjusting?

(She smiles, but the **MASS** *roars and jerks. He steps back.)*

Aww, you don't know whether to stand your ground or try to run? That's because you can't really see me. If you could really see me, you'd know what to do.

BUCK. I can see you.

OBAKE. Of course, where would you run?

(The **MASS** *writhes behind her. He can almost see it.)*

BUCK. They're, they're coming for me, my team; they'll find me [down here.]

OBAKE. [Ah yes, the] architect is missing. Where is Mr. Mason? They'll have to find him, won't they?

BUCK. That's right.

OBAKE. Well then, we should talk now so you can get back to your grand building. What will it be? The building?

BUCK. The building?

OBAKE. Please don't make me repeat myself. It's tiresome.

BUCK. A hotel.

OBAKE. Oh, that's perfect. That's perfect. Hmmm, I'll let you go back architect, but I need something from you first, a certain consideration. I need you to move your hotel, ugh that word, the idea of it, it's so perfect. I need you to move it a bit, so that it's above me, just here.

(She points up.)

BUCK. Why would I ever [agree to....]

OBAKE. [Because I'm] asking nicely instead of skinning you and that's more than enough, quite enough.

BUCK. Do you, I'm not sure you understand what you're asking for here; do you have any idea how much work that [would entail?]

OBAKE. [Don't be impolite!] I wouldn't like that and you might suddenly find yourself in a pool of blood with your skull crushed into pieces. But, no, just listen to me, how silly. Look, you give me what I want, and really its not so much, and then I'll make the thing you want most in the world happen for you.

BUCK. A strange woman in a hole granting wishes?

OBAKE. Strange? Oh no, Buck, you'd be amazed.

BUCK. Well, your offer sounds too good to be true, as far as offers go. Which is absolutely my politest possible way of saying it sounds like a trick.

OBAKE. No, it sounds like a bargain. That's what I do. I get what I want and then I give you the thing you want most, no matter what it is. And let's be frank with each other, it's never money or love. Everyone thinks they'd wish for money or love. Or success, but just look at you; you already have those things. Look at the buildings that you create, spiraling above the city; temporary, but beautiful.

BUCK. My buildings will last forever. No one does what I do; no one can do what I do. My buildings are monuments of design.

OBAKE. Huh, I'm familiar with your work, Buck.

BUCK. Then you know I'm telling [the truth.]

OBAKE. [And I know] I can give you what you want, Buck.

BUCK. Stop saying my name.

OBAKE. Anything you want, Buck.

BUCK. I want to get out of this hole.

OBAKE. That's not it.

BUCK. It absolutely is it, that's what [I want.]

OBAKE. [That's immediate,] that's not something from deep inside. And nothing about your life will be the same after our little chat, so why not ask for something more? Let me hear that hidden, secret thing you've always wanted, let me see it, the thing you've never told anyone. Let it just slip into your head without editing or thought…

(She brightens and takes a pointed step away from him before clapping her hands onto her chest. The **MASS** *exhales.)*

Ah. There it is. That's not very nice at all, is it?

BUCK. What? I didn't [even…]

OBAKE. [Oh yes, I] see it in you.

BUCK. I don't know what you think you saw, but I don't have any secrets. My life is an open book and there have been so many articles about me already, everyone knows my past and it is spotless. Now listen, I don't want anything that I'm not willing to work for, to earn.

MASS. *(in whispers, hushed, not in unison…)* "Little girls."

OBAKE. You and I will get along just fine I think.

BUCK. You don't know anything about me.

OBAKE. Little. Girls.

BUCK. I'm not interested in your bargain.

(The **OBAKE** *smiles.)*

OBAKE. Are you sure?

BUCK. I do not want anything from you!

(Moans and a roar rise up from the **MASS** *behind the* **OBAKE.***)*

OBAKE. You presume too much by yelling.

(pause)

You will accept my offer and you will do what I wish. And this building will be a crowning achievement. Your life will be full, you'll have that one awful thing you so desperately want even if you won't name it out loud and then one day, when your building falls, you'll end up back down here with me.

(She suddenly grabs him by the throat and forces him down.)

Or would you prefer I just eat you now, chew your bones and feel your flesh sliding down my throat.

BUCK. How is this a bargain if I have to accept the terms, how is that a deal?

OBAKE. Semantics.

BUCK. No, you called yourself a bargainer.

(She releases him and backs away.)

OBAKE. Threatening someone is a perfectly legitimate bargaining tactic. And I call myself all sorts of things, spirit, ghost, other, but right now the descriptive words that come to mind are impatient and famished.

BUCK. What choice do I have?

OBAKE. Now there you go again, Buck, you always have a choice. In fact, I can almost taste your "choice" from here. Please, please be selfless. It's a delicious quality.

BUCK. Just, just stay over there.

OBAKE. Is that right?

BUCK. Stay away from me.

OBAKE. You've lost a bit of that bravado now, haven't you? Don't worry, Buck Mason. I'd rather get my price than a simple meal. Because your hotel will be my playground, a playground for "people" like me. And I think we both know that's a stretch, don't we? But honestly, between you and me, no one really pays much attention.

(Pause. Then quietly...)

BUCK. I shouldn't want what I want.

OBAKE. Hmmm, it's not so uncommon. I mean, it's awful. But really that's a moral judgment and I don't often have a place for that kind of thinking. Trust me when I tell you there are worse things. There are much worse things.

BUCK. Awful. It is awful. This can't be, you can't be real.

OBAKE. I'd wager everything feels unreal to you right now. Let's find out together, shall we?

(pause)

BUCK. Deal.

(She laughs and claps a bit, enjoying the moment.)

OBAKE. Good. Now, they'll find you soon; drag you back up to the light. I can hear them digging, those gigantic machines. Who could ever get used to such disgusting things? Everywhere. You know, I don't miss a thing about the world up there. Except the moon.

*(She looks up and the **MASS** seems to wilt around her with wonder and awe at something unseen.)*

I do miss the moon. So beautiful. But nothing else.

BUCK. I can't remember the last time I even looked at the moon.

OBAKE. Such a shame to take something so lovely for granted.

BUCK. *(quietly...)* A shame.

OBAKE. I should go.

BUCK. Go where?

OBAKE. Deeper. Don't worry, I'll be around.

(The **OBAKE** *steps back to the edge of the circle with a smile on her face. She offers a little wave and is suddenly grappled by many pairs of hands erupting from the* **MASS** *behind her. But she stops and turns back, the hands releasing her and waiting.)*

Oh…and Buck? When I see you again, I'll kill you. So try your very, very best not to see me.

(She turns again allowing the hands to envelop her, pulling her into the mass. She vanishes from the circle and **BUCK** *is left alone.)*

End Scene

ii. dreadful parlor games

(The central "living room" area of a large hotel suite.
JASPER *and* **SAM** *stand chatting near some luggage.)*

(In one corner, **KAMI 1** *stands very still. She is in a
simple, drab outfit, perhaps a bit dirty, hands clasped
in front of her.* **KAMI 2** *stands behind her looming just
over her left shoulder. Also drab and dirty. His hands
are clasped behind his back. They both stare at the men
intensely. They are incredibly still. Nothing else. Only
staring.)*

JASPER. Look, Sam, I didn't want to say anything in front of
Kimberly, she's clearly already annoyed that I'm here.
But [what was…]

SAM. [Not true.] She's really glad you came. We got a dis-
count on the hotel suite by having more than two
people. So…that's good.

JASPER. Uh huh. She pushes my buttons on purpose and
you know it.

SAM. What did you not want to say in front of her?

JASPER. When we stopped for gas that last time, what
was the deal with her really obviously trying to drive
off and leave me in the middle of nowhere? We all
laughed and "ha ha" and whatever, but [that was…]

SAM. [She just,] she just didn't know you were still inside.
She thought you were in the back seat.

JASPER. She waved goodbye.

SAM. Come on.

JASPER. She hates me, right?

SAM. When we checked into the hotel, were you paying
attention to that elevator operator guy? Because it is
completely crazy how much you look like that elevator
operator guy.

SAM. What are you talking about?

JASPER. It was eerie.

SAM. Eerie? Okay first, that guy was a weirdo. Second, I don't look anything like him.

JASPER. So much like him.

(**KAMI** 1 *and* **KAMI** 2 *shuffle forward a bit. Barely a foot, but they inch closer.*)

JASPER. Third, I'm trying to talk to you, but fine. If you don't want to talk about why your girlfriend tried to abandon me at a Mobil station in the middle of the night, a rainy night, with nothing but a little bag of beef jerky and some Red Bull, then we'll just wait until she gets back with the ice and I'll ask her directly.

SAM. You said you didn't want to annoy her.

JASPER. You said she's happy I'm here.

SAM. Jasper, she…that's right.

JASPER. So that was amazingly convincing. Let's just unpack.

SAM. Look, you're always going to be my best friend. I mean, unless you do something like rob me or burn my house down or commit [some…]

JASPER. [What if] it's an accident?

SAM. What?

JASPER. What if I burn your house down and it's accidental?

SAM. This "moment" is exactly the kind of thing that gets under Kimberly's [skin, Jasper.]

JASPER. [I feel like] intent is important.

SAM. I'm saying it would be bad if you burn my house down on purpose, willfully, that would be bad. If it's an accident then of course that's not going to, just, I'm trying to say you're always gonna be my friend. But Kimberly is really special, man. I think she might be the one. Like, "the one." And it just makes me so fucking tired the way you [two bicker.]

JASPER. [Okay, ya' know,] I love that you have a girlfriend and you're in love and blah, blah, blah. I mean, I want those things for [you, obviously.]

SAM. [Blah, blah,] blah?

JASPER. She's, whatever, she's great. But you act differently around her.

SAM. I am different around her.

JASPER. Well then don't act like there's nothing different. And don't act like she likes me when she doesn't.

SAM. She just doesn't get your sense of humor, that's all. Because your sense of humor is like getting hit in the knee by a really weird sledgehammer. And don't you make that face at me; you know I'm right. And I love it. I think you're a riot. Mostly. But it's definitely an acquired taste. So here's the deal: I'll make sure we all get along, no matter how fucking exhausting, I'll do my very best. And you just have to promise to be good.

JASPER. I hear you.

SAM. I want your word. Say, "I promise."

JASPER. "I promise."

SAM. Good. And she'll be good, too. I promise for her. In fact, I'm sure she'll be fine since you have your own part of the suite. This is massive.

JASPER. That's fair. All right.

SAM. I can't get over the size of the room.

JASPER. It is kind of a creepy hotel though, don't you think?

SAM. We have a bar and a living room in our suite, let it be creepy.

(*JASPER goes rigid and then blank as* **KAMI 1** *starts speaking intensely under her breath. His mouth moves and he speaks, but it's as if he's speaking for her.*)

JASPER (**KAMI 1**). Don't call it a living room.

SAM. Why not?

JASPER (**KAMI 1**). Don't call it a living room.

SAM. That's what it's, what is wrong with you, your eyes are [all out of…]

(**KAMI 2** *begins to hum a spiritual or church song from the early Twentieth Century underneath the speaking.*)

JASPER (KAMI 1). [Don't call it] a living room. A living room is a misnomer meant to erase the stench of death. Homes used to have a parlor. Good homes. And the parlor was for entertaining guests but it was also for displaying family members after they passed away, a room for coffins, a room for mourning and visitation.

SAM. Are you [serious?]

JASPER (KAMI 1). [But then in] the 1920s, Ladies' Home Journal encouraged American women, "Don't let you parlor be a dying room. Instead, treat it like a living room." Trust me, I had the issue, I remember it like it was yesterday.

SAM. Um, okay, you're starting to freak [me out.]

(**KAMI 2** *raises his left hand out, palm up.* **JASPER** *completes the same motion as if being pulled along.*)

[So a living] room isn't what you think and this collection of well-appointed furniture, no matter how well intentioned shouldn't be a called a "living room." Ever. Ever. Ever!

(**KIMBERLY** *enters with an empty ice bucket.* **KAMI 1** *stops speaking abruptly as* **KAMI 2** *lowers his arm and stops singing.* **JASPER** *is suddenly present and at ease again.*)

KIMBERLY. I couldn't find an ice machine.

JASPER. Should have let me go.

KIMBERLY. You wouldn't have found one either, I even looked on other floors. And this hotel is deserted. Even for the middle of the night there is no one else here.

SAM. They're just, just in their rooms. Asleep. We checked in really late.

KIMBERLY. And the other guests didn't. Because they didn't let their pal have control of the map.

JASPER. Here we go.

KIMBERLY. I'm not saying anything. It's raining. Dark. I'm sure it was hard to see the tall, gigantic, well-lit hotel on the map. Driving past it. Three times.

JASPER. Stop it.

KIMBERLY. I'm not doing anything.

SAM. Kimberly, don't pick fights. Jasper, are you all right?

JASPER. I'm fine, why?

KIMBERLY. He's fine. Oh, I don't know if you noticed it, Jasper, but it's super eerie how much that Elevator Operator looks like you.

JASPER. False.

SAM. Wow. That's exactly what I said, "eerie." Isn't that what I said, Jasper?

JASPER. I do not look like that guy.

KIMBERLY. So much like that guy.

JASPER. What the fuck are you talking about?

SAM. Jasper, you promised you were going to be on your best behavior.

JASPER. This is me being on my best behavior.

SAM. And Kimberly, you could be several degrees nicer.

KIMBERLY. Oh, you guys won't believe what that elevator operator who looks like Jasper told me about this room. I think I know why we got such a deal. According to him, several people have died in this room.

JASPER. No way.

KIMBERLY. Several. That's what he said.

JASPER. Liar.

SAM. Jasper.

JASPER. She's totally baiting me.

KIMBERLY. And they all died by hanging. Ooooooooooh.

(She laughs.)

Or being hanged. Or hung. It can't be hung. Whatever. It could be kind of cool, I guess. To stay in a room of death, a room that's probably haunted by spirits that are watching us, quietly, waiting to see what we'll do. Waiting to see if they'll have to kill us! Can you imagine?

JASPER. Sam, please tell you girlfriend to cool it with the bullshit scary stories.

SAM. If I tell her to cool it, and there's no guarantee she'll listen...

(**KIMBERLY** *laughs.*)

Then will you promise not to do the Ladies' Home Journal thing again?

JASPER. Kimberly, please tell your boyfriend to speak English.

KIMBERLY. You've got your own room right over there.

JASPER. Because you already need couple time? We just got here.

KIMBERLY. I'm simply saying that if you don't want to hang out with us here in our, heh, in our spacious living room, please feel free to go away and give us some privacy.

(*She nuzzles next to* **SAM.** **JASPER** *goes rigid again and then blank as* **KAMI 1** *starts speaking intensely under her breath and* **KAMI 2** *starts humming another tune.*)

JASPER (KAMI 1). Don't call it a living room. It's so very, very thoughtless and rude. Thoughtless and rude.

KIMBERLY. Excuse me?

SAM. No, this is what I was talking about. This happened when you were looking for ice.

JASPER (KAMI 1). That issue of Ladies' Home Journal was read to me. It was read to me and I remember it. Read to me. "Don't let your parlor be a dying room. Instead, make it a living room."

KIMBERLY. Ladies' Home Journal. Seriously?

SAM. I have no idea.

JASPER (KAMI 1). I need to find some rope and teach you some manners.

KIMBERLY. Jasper!

(**SAM** *takes a step closer and waves his hand in front of* **JASPER**'s *face with no reaction at all.*)

SAM. It's like he's gone or something.

JASPER (KAMI 1). I need to find some rope and teach you some manners.

(As they speak, KAMI 2 shuffles forward in the same odd, clipped step, barely picking up his feet, moving near JASPER.)

KIMBERLY. Okay, this is totally something you guys cooked up while I was gone, right? You can both fuck off.

SAM. I swear to god, I have absolutely no idea what is going on.

JASPER (KAMI 1). I need to find some rope and teach you some manners.

KIMBERLY. Come here; get away from him.

SAM. He's not going to hurt me. He's our best friend.

KIMBERLY. He's your best friend. Jasper, quit it. It's not funny, okay. Sammy, I told you not to bring him. Is this, what, supposed to be funny?

SAM. Seriously, this is not the way to kick off the trip.

(KAMI 2 suddenly bends forward at the waist, head cocked to the side, staring at the couple. JASPER also abruptly bends forward at the waist and, eyes wide, opens his mouth in a scream. No sound comes out, but the intensity is there, and SAM and KIMBERLY are knocked to the ground.)

(KAMI 2 begins speaking at full voice as JASPER continues to scream in silence.)

KAMI 2. It's cold, it's colder than you could ever, and this is ours, you don't get to, this is ours, we can't leave and you can't stay because this thing, this one thing, and if you knew what we had to go through to, this is our room! You don't have any business in this room, no, colder than, no business, too cold, too dark for your kind of, too loud, you're noisy, disturbing all of the, and if you don't leave now, leave now, leave now, you won't leave at all. You won't leave at all! You won't, we can't, our room, had to go through, no business, you can't stay here –

*(As he speaks, **KAMI 1** shuffles over to him and gently places her hand on his shoulder. This causes him to stop abruptly and return to a neutral, quiet standing position. She then steps in front of him again recreating their original pose.)*

KIMBERLY. What fuck was that?

SAM. I don't know.

KIMBERLY. I want to leave.

SAM. What about Jasper?

KIMBERLY. I want to leave right now.

SAM. We can't just leave him here like some kind of zombie.

KIMBERLY. Yes we can! I tried to leave him at the Mobil station, I can sure as hell leave [him here.]

SAM. [I'm not] leaving.

*(**KAMI 2** starts up with his song again, only this time at full voice. **SAM** and **KIMBERLY** can hear it now.)*

KIMBERLY. Okay, this is fucked up.

SAM. Where is it even coming from?

KIMBERLY. This is not okay, Sam, I'm getting out of here.

*(**KAMI 1** begins to inhale sharply, repeatedly, almost as if she's trying to catch her breath. **SAM** and **KIMBERLY** begin to clutch at their throats, gasping for air, staggering around and eventually collapsing. **KAMI 2** gets louder as **SAM** and **KIMBERLY** fall to the ground. **KAMI 1** continues the sharp inhalations.)*

*(Suddenly everything stops. **SAM** and **KIMBERLY** are lifeless on the ground. **JASPER** is still facing them. After a moment, **KAMI 1** turns to **KAMI 2** and begins speaking under her breath...)*

JASPER (KAMI 1). I'll find some rope to teach them some manners.

KAMI 2. Strong rope.

JASPER (KAMI 1). I'll find some rope to teach them some manners.

KAMI 2. This is our room.

JASPER (KAMI 1). We'll hang them up.

KAMI 2. That's what we do.

JASPER (KAMI 1). Yes.

> (KAMI 2 *kisses* KAMI 1 *on the cheek.* KAMI 1 *smiles.*
> JASPER *is still blank, facing the bodies of his friends.*)

KAMI 2. I love you.

JASPER (KAMI 1). I love you, too.

End Scene

iii. bleach & other
household cleaners

(**BETTY** *sits on one side of an immense hole in the floor. Wearing rubber gloves, she vigorously scrubs at the edge with a wire sponge. Her hair is pulled back, but has come undone. Some bottles of cleaning solution sit next to her.*)

(*In "the hole," the ensemble is huddled to form a* **MASS,** *lying on the floor, curled up with each other.*)

(**ETHAN** *enters.*)

ETHAN. Betty, are you awake? I thought for sure you'd still be out cold this, holy shit! What the hell happened? Betty, what happened to the floor?!

BETTY. I'm cleaning it up.

ETHAN. Betty there is a giant hole in the kitchen floor.

    (*pause*)

There's, okay, there's a huge fucking hole in the [floor.]

BETTY. [Ethan,] do I look stupid, am I stupid Ethan? I'm on my knees right next to the thing; I know there's a hole in the kitchen floor. But I'm trying to clean it up and it just keeps getting bigger.

    (*She breaks off a small piece of the floor and squeezes it.*)

ETHAN. I don't think that's helping.

BETTY. Huh, well, I don't think you know what you're talking about.

ETHAN. Jesus! That was harsh, this is just [a little...]

BETTY. [Oh, was] it harsh?

ETHAN. Yes. Betty, how did this happen? This is not normal.

BETTY. It's not normal? Oh, I thought maybe every night when I take all of those fucking pills to go to sleep, giant holes just open up in the kitchen floor. No? That's not how it happens? Obviously it's not normal, Ethan. I've never seen anything like this in my life. But I've been trying to wrap my head around all kinds of things I never imagined before last night, last night when I didn't take those pills.

ETHAN. You're supposed to take your pills, Betty, the [doctor said…]

BETTY. [And I didn't] go to sleep.

ETHAN. Why didn't you take them?

BETTY. So I've had time and I'm just a little more used to the idea of the hole than you right now, okay?

ETHAN. Okay, I'm gonna need a little bit more than that.

BETTY. Oh? Fine. I started trying to clean off this "stain" in the middle of the floor last night. This stain. And it wouldn't come up. And the harder I scrubbed, all night, the deeper in it went until…

ETHAN. Until what?

BETTY. Until now, do I need to draw you a map? And I'm trying really hard Ethan, I mean really hard to stay calm and focused, to give you the benefit of the, I don't know, but you really need to get out.

ETHAN. You want me to leave? Okay. So I don't know exactly what to call the way you're acting right now, but it's giving me "concern" and then there's also the gigantic hole in the floor and I'm not going anywhere.

BETTY. Well, stay away from the hole, because I don't know how big it'll get.

ETHAN. Wait, wait, so all night you've been, wait, did you do this?

BETTY. Ugh, I'll tell you what Ethan, it's a question of perspective I guess. But I'm sure to you it seems like I did this, so yes, I did this.

ETHAN. Okay, what?

BETTY. Do you think there are things that defy cleaning, in the face of modern chemicals designed to clean anything? I don't like that idea at all, but I don't know if this will ever be clean, it just seems to get worse and worse, but it has to be cleaned and I think maybe I'm losing it [a little.]

ETHAN. [Oh no, no, don't] cry, I have no idea what's going on, but I wanna' help if I can, just, I still don't understand [what's…]

BETTY. [You stay] over there!

> *(He stops abruptly and takes a few steps back.)*

> Just stay over there. I don't know how much weight the floor can…

> *(**ETHAN** moves to the edge of the hole and looks in.)*

> Or, ya' know, go right up to the edge. Ignore me and go up to the edge.

ETHAN. Jesus. I can't even see the bottom.

> *(She is scrubbing again…)*

> Betty, I can't even see [the bottom.]

BETTY. [It doesn't] have a bottom!

> *(She tosses the piece of floor into the hole. The **MUD WOMAN** catches it, so it makes no sound.)*

> I was surprised when I realized that, it just goes and goes and goes. Can you imagine?

ETHAN. How can it not have a bottom?

BETTY. Ethan, do you think I'm a good wife, despite my issues, insomnia, nightmares, anxiety, have I been a, you know what, don't answer that.
ETHAN. So I'm gonna, I think we should, I'm gonna' call someone.

BETTY. Tell me who you call for something like this please. Please tell me. A general contractor? A physics professor?

ETHAN. Your doctor.

BETTY. Perfect! Perfect, so he can give me more fucking pills.

ETHAN. Well just stop making it worse.

> *(She laughs at him and keeps scrubbing.)*

BETTY. Do you know what it's been all week, the nightmare?

ETHAN. That's why you're supposed to take [your pills.]

BETTY. [Ugh, I have the nightmares] either way, the pills just stop me from waking up.

(She stops scrubbing.)

I'm underwater, like standing at the bottom of some kind of, it's deep, it's murky, but I look up and I can see through the wavy water there are lights. So I try to stand up and I'm so much larger than I should be, like when I stand up, my head and shoulder break the surface and I keep getting bigger. And when I'm finally standing up, my hands are all scaly with horrible hook-like things. They're not my hands, they shouldn't be anything's hands. And I look towards the lights and you know what they are? Clusters of buildings, a city maybe, and bam, right there, right in front of me is that awful hotel where we stayed on our honeymoon. Do you remember it?

ETHAN. Of course.

BETTY. Because it was awful.

ETHAN. You've only slept through a handful of nights in all the years since we [stayed there.]

BETTY. [Somewhere] underneath all of the modern furniture and the little bottles of liquor. Say it was awful; say that.

ETHAN. It was awful.

BETTY. And in that entire awful hotel, there's only one light on. One room. I'm bigger than the entire building, it's dark, it's raining, I'm not supposed to be there, I know I'm not supposed to be there and just the one light is on in one room and as I take a gigantic step towards the hotel, somewhere, so small, I can hear someone screaming.

ETHAN. That's a terrible dream.

BETTY. Awful.

ETHAN. And I'm sorry you have to have it.

BETTY. So I didn't take my pills to sleep. Last night, I didn't take them.

ETHAN. I heard you.

BETTY. I didn't go to sleep, Ethan.

ETHAN. I get it.

BETTY. So I was awake all night, Ethan.

ETHAN. I didn't…oh.

BETTY. I saw you with that woman on the table, I saw, against the counter, I saw, and here on the floor. I saw that, all of it here on the floor. How could I not see it? I even walked in here at one point, stood right there, and you didn't even see me.

ETHAN. Listen, baby, I know how it [might seem…]

BETTY. [Ugh, don't] call me that. It makes my skin crawl. Look, I asked you to leave, can you leave? Clearly I have a lot of work to do and I don't really have time to answer all of your questions about the unprecedented and admittedly bizarre hole in the kitchen floor.

(A beautiful voice rises from the hole, distant but clear.)

MUD WOMAN. I love you Ethan.

BETTY. You shut-up down there, do you hear me!

ETHAN. Is, is someone down there?

MUD WOMAN. I love you Ethan.

*(**BETTY** begins pouring bleach into the hole.)*

BETTY. You would think, with all these chemicals, I mean really.

ETHAN. Okay, that time I heard it, who's down there?

BETTY. No one. Would I be pouring bleach onto a person? No. And how could there be a person in the bottom-less pit that is now our kitchen floor? There couldn't. There couldn't be a bottomless hole and there couldn't be a person in the bottomless hole, now really, what a lovely morning we've had and I really should have made coffee and I wonder how many nights when I was out cold you did things on this floor that I can't clean and could you get the hell out!?!

(A mud-covered hand abruptly rises from the hole.)

God [damn it!]

MUD WOMAN. [I love you] Ethan.

ETHAN. What the fuck?!

BETTY. You stay down there!

(**BETTY** *kicks at the hand until it disappears back into the hole.* **ETHAN** *backs away further, trips and falls into a seated position. She returns to pouring bleach.*)

ETHAN. That was a person, was that a person?

BETTY. No, it's just dirt.

ETHAN. That was a fucking hand.

BETTY. Fine.

ETHAN. Fine? Fine what?

BETTY. If you saw a hand, that's what you saw. How many women do you think? If you had a guess, how many nights?

ETHAN. Betty, it just happened, I want to explain it to you, but this doesn't seem like [the best...]

BETTY. [Please] explain it.

ETHAN. Betty, that was a hand. Can we [just...]

BETTY. [Explain!]

ETHAN. Okay, okay, I know you've been sad, but I don't know how to help. And you haven't touched me in months, I'm not saying it's your fault, it's not your fault, but you take all of that stuff and pass out and it's hard to sleep next to you like that. You don't even move. It's creepy, but I know you need the rest, I'm not blaming you. So I started to get up sometimes. Then I started to go out sometimes. Then I started to come back sometimes.

BETTY. So more than just last night.

ETHAN. I don't ever bring them here. Usually.

BETTY. Is that a yes?

ETHAN. I take them, I mostly go to that motel by the interstate, or just, in the car, but you're always out cold, so I thought, no, no, I don't want you to think I come here and do that to [you because...]

BETTY. [You did] come here and do that.

MUD WOMAN. I love you Ethan.

(**BETTY** *starts laughing pointedly when she hears the voice.*)

ETHAN. Betty, let's just get out of here. Let's get you away from whatever that is and then I'll explain everything, just [let...]

BETTY. [No.]

MUD WOMAN. I love you Ethan.

ETHAN. Look, baby, we [were both...]

BETTY. [I told] you not to call me that!

ETHAN. I was a dick, I was wrong and I'm sorry you saw what you saw, no, that I did what I did, but let's get the hell out of here.

(*The hand reappears, groping the edge of the hole for a grip.*)

MUD WOMAN. I love you Ethan.

ETHAN. Oh my god, what is that?

(*The **MUD WOMAN**, pulls herself out of the hole. Keeping her stomach on the floor, she writhes to move.*)

BETTY. That's me. See how pretty.

ETHAN. Make it go back in the hole.

BETTY. I can't.

ETHAN. Make it go back in the hole, Betty!

BETTY. I've tried, but I can't. She just keeps climbing back out. I think she's maybe all the parts that fell out of me when I saw you last night fucking that other woman in the middle of the floor.

MUD WOMAN. I love you Ethan.

ETHAN. Don't let it [touch you.]

BETTY. [I know it's] only trust, right? Only love. Only you fucking another woman, or women, how would I even know? So I should have a proportional response. But if I could crush your skull right now, I might. If I could twist your arms back until the bones inside buckle and shatter, I might. If I could peel off your skin a piece at a time, I would. I mean, at this rate...

(She pulls off her wedding ring and throws it into the hole. Again, the MUD WOMAN *catches it before it falls.)*

ETHAN. Don't!

MUD WOMAN. I love you Ethan.

BETTY. This is my house, my fucking kitchen! You don't get [to...]

ETHAN. [This is] our house!

BETTY. Oh! Our house?

ETHAN. Yes!

BETTY. Okay, you can have this part! This part right here. All this is yours. Just jump right in, it's all yours and you can...

(The MUD WOMAN *gets close enough to touch* BETTY. *She grabs* BETTY*'s leg and it immediately stops* BETTY, *her eyes blank.)*

ETHAN. Betty?

(A low hum softly fills the kitchen with vibration. Both women's heads tilt up and BETTY *inhales sharply. The* MUD WOMAN *pulls herself up against* BETTY*'s leg.* BETTY *looks as if she might float into the air if not for the anchor of the* MUD WOMAN. *The words spill out of them both in a torrent.)*

BETTY. I don't think you can know how much joy I feel when you touch me, when I feel you caress me, that's love, such love, your lips, touching my lips, it moves through me like waves, like it might pick me [up...]

MUD WOMAN. [No.]

BETTY. And I feel you press against me, against me, this pressure, your arms around me, breath on my neck, never [anything like it...]

MUD WOMAN. [No, don't! Let] [go.]

BETTY. [And every time] you are so gentle, lay me back on the bed, I feel you inside me and my eyes go wide, head thrown back and every part of me can feel every small thing in the air, moves [against me...]

MUD WOMAN. [Stop!]

BETTY. Every thing that moves anywhere and the sweat and heavy breathing and you [and me and every little thing as my heads starts to spin and I can't be still, it feels so amazing...]

MUD WOMAN. [You're a liar and you lied, you cheated, you ruined, you're a ruiner and I watched you ruin!]

(**BETTY** *kicks free of the* **MUD WOMAN** *and falls backwards onto the floor. The* **MUD WOMAN**, *face down, reaches towards her.*)

MUD WOMAN. I love you Ethan.

ETHAN. Shut-up! Shut the fuck up you thing! Betty, Betty, are you all right?

BETTY. No.

ETHAN. Look, just, just don't think about last night, what you saw, think about all beautiful moments, mornings in bed, when I brush the hair back from your face, not even beautiful, just the everyday stuff, the little things that are us. When we go to coffee shop and just sit quietly for hours and we'll look up every once in a while and just smile. I know your face like that, it's right here. The things that [aren't...]

MUD WOMAN. [I love] you Ethan.

ETHAN. Why won't it stop saying that?! What if I, what if I make it go back?

BETTY. You can't make it go back [down there.]

ETHAN. [No? What if] I fucking kill it? I can throw it back down there if it's dead, if it's dead it'll fucking stay down there. It can't keep repeating that.

MUD WOMAN. I love you [Ethan.]

ETHAN. [You're going] back down there, you're going to leave us alone.

(**ETHAN** *leaps across the hole and lands next to the* **MUD WOMAN**, *grabbing her. She immediately wraps around him like some kind of vice.* **ETHAN** *grapples to get the* **MUD WOMAN** *to release.*)

MUD WOMAN. I love you Ethan I love you Ethan I love you
Ethan I [love you Ethan.]

ETHAN. [Ah! No! Get] off of me!

BETTY. Ethan!

(They both fall into the hole, disappearing. Silent.)

BETTY. Ethan? Ethan? I wish you'd left when I said to leave.

*(She sits for a moment at the edge of the hole. She begins
to scrub the edge of the hole again. A woman's hand cov-
ered in mud abruptly jerks out of the hole.)*

MUD WOMAN. I love you Ethan.

BETTY. Shhh, I know you did.

(Pause. She continues cleaning.)

MUD WOMAN. I love you Ethan.

BETTY. I know.

End Scene

iv. an unfortunate
storm related mishap

(EDITH *stands in the center of the circle. An out dated suitcase sits by her side. She's forcing a smile, but she's nervous.*)

(*Just outside of the circle, barely lit, the* OBAKE *sits in a chair. Her legs crossed, her posture above reproach. She listens but is focused on sewing something on a remnant of fabric. The* MASS *behind her is focused on* EDITH.)

EDITH. I'm not a very good "vacationer." If there even is such a word, but you know what I mean, right? I'm not good at going somewhere just for the sake of relaxing. Never have been. But Henry, that's my husband, he insisted on taking a trip to the beach. He said we'd earned it. I've never been one to argue with him, I learned that one pretty quickly. Isn't it disappointing how you can think you know a person and then everything goes all lopsided.

He never hit me or anything, that's not where this is going. He just could have been nicer in some ways. In retrospect though, between you and me, I didn't really want to go.

(*The* OBAKE *chuckles to herself as the* MASS *all lean back.*)

But before I knew it, we were in a strange room in a strange city, not too far from the beach. Such a shame though, it rained every day from the minute we arrived, just rain and rain. That silly kind of rain that's not really rain but still just enough to get you wet, you know the kind.

I didn't mind staying in the hotel mostly, I guess there's something about other people cleaning and cooking for you that does feel a little bit luxurious. Although I was stunned when I found out how much money Henry was spending on that place. Stunned. But I liked the room well enough. Henry was livid.

And angry. He drank everything in the mini-bar. And then a nice woman named Vanessa, I think that was her name, would come each morning and refill it so he could drink it all again. I stopped looking at the prices on the little menu card. He didn't want to hear about it anyway.

EDITH. *(cont.)* So that was pretty much the first two days. There was some sex, but…eh, it wasn't very good. There was some relaxing, but you could always hear the rain outside. There was some name-calling and that wasn't very nice. And the little bottles of rum and gin everywhere. Then on the third night, after I finished building the cutest little sandcastle, well that's not what to call it, but I built something like a sandcastle out of those little liquor bottles, the rain became something else all together. I mean, it really just transformed into a big storm. Not a hurricane, they weren't evacuating, but those sirens kept going off every few hours.

(The **OBAKE** *begins to sing quietly to herself…)*

After this attractive young man named Grant from room service delivered an impulsively ordered snack for the two of us, we went to bed. But the storm got louder, I don't know, just battering the windows. That's how it sounded. I have no idea how Henry managed to sleep through it. Well, he was drunk so that's probably why. Also, those decongestants probably made him drowsy. Anyway, I finally got up and opened the curtains covering the floor-to-ceiling windows.

(The **MASS** *slams to the floor with making a collective thud with their hands, releasing a hissing noise as* **EDITH***'s eyes go wide.)*

The rain was almost sideways, because of the wind, and coming down in these thick sheets. We were up so high, I could see pockets of the area between our hotel and the ocean were without electricity. Just dark spots here and there where the power had gone out and then past that, the emergency lights out by the beach.

EDITH. *(cont.)* And beyond that, out in the water, something moving. At first it was just waves pushed around by the storm, but then definitely something moving. It was so dark, I pressed my face against the glass and I saw…

(She stops, wiping away tears and catching herself. She smiles nervously, recovering. The **OBAKE** *stops singing.)*

Now, I know how this sounds so don't think I'm unaware, all right?

(She looks around to see if anyone else is listening. The **OBAKE** *stops her sewing and focuses on* **EDITH.***)*

But this thing, that's what I'm going to call it, this thing started rising out of the water. It was hard to make it out against the night sky, the details, but the storm clouds provided a kind of backdrop, so I could see it in relief. A bit. I've never, it was so large with a long neck, not long, just stretched somehow and it had these, I'm not going to say hands, because that would make it real in my head. It was gigantic, larger than the hotel even, can you imagine? And then it took a step towards the shore. I just started screaming.

(The **MASS** *starts screaming, but the* **OBAKE** *puts out her hands and quiets them, never letting her gaze leave* **EDITH.***)*

I rushed into back to the bed, but Henry was still out cold. I didn't know what to do. He wouldn't wake up, I pushed him, yelling, but he just wouldn't budge. I looked around, frantic, for something to hit him with. I grabbed one of those little coffee pots from the table in the room and stood over him with it in my hand. He was breathing, heavy. Not snoring, breathing heavy. And I just, I just…

(The **OBAKE** *leans forward and takes over with something like zealous enthusiasm as* **EDITH** *relives every moment of the story in her mind, across her face.)*

OBAKE. I pulled back and smashed the coffee pot over his head, but it didn't break the first time, or the second, so I kept slamming it down over and over until it shattered and even then I kept bringing it down, jagged edges and all until I couldn't even see what I was hitting anymore and I couldn't even breathe, everything spinning, slamming it down again and again with that image of the thing in the storm looming just out of sight so I couldn't make it out exactly, something slipped, something undone, slamming, cutting, beating, just beating and I...

(EDITH *cries out causing the* **OBAKE** *to stop. They are both out of breath, chests heaving. The* **OBAKE** *leans back, delighted, trying to compose herself.* **EDITH** *looks broken, but tries to pull herself back together. This takes a moment.*)

EDITH. I didn't like Henry, he was my husband but I didn't like him. Even still, there was no reason, not that there ever could be a reason for that kind of, I just have no idea what happened. I had this broken coffee pot in my hand and he was lying in the bed, wet sheets. But before I could even think about it, the storm shattered the windows in our room, rain pouring in and I fell backward as the wind swept through, knocking over furniture, shaking the room. Henry's body rolled off the bed and just disappeared over the edge of the broken window. Just gone. I dragged myself to the edge and looked over. His body had fallen all the way down and hit the concrete next to the pool. I could barely see it in the floodlights next to the emergency exit. It looked like several rooms had shattered windows on the lower floors and suddenly I became aware that my hands were being cut by the edges where the windows broke.

(She looks at her hands. The **OBAKE** looks at her own hands. The **MASS** behind the **OBAKE** hisses and moans quietly, but she silences them with a sharp gesture.)

EDITH. *(cont.)* Everyone was evacuated to the basement. That's where a very understanding paramedic named Jonathan bandaged my hands. Over hot chocolate, he told me several people had died because of flying debris or from falling. So there were other people who had…difficulties. The funny thing, well none of this is really funny, but the odd thing, one of the odd things, is that even now I have trouble being sad about Henry. I hate what happened, but there's some kind of fog around him in my head. It's almost like he never existed.

(The **OBAKE** *begins sewing again with a grin and begins to sing quietly to herself again…)*

Oh, but everyone at the hotel was so nice about everything, so apologetic. Like they could control the weather. They told me I could come back and stay anytime in the future, if that wouldn't be too painful. But I don't think I'll ever go back there. I'm not much of a "vacationer" anyway. Did I already mention that?

End Scene

v. hearts & flowers

(GINGER is waiting in a low-key party dress. She gently sings "Dream a Little Dream" to herself and gently tests out a few dance steps.)

*(On the edge of the circle, **SHIKIGAMI 1** and **SHIKIGAMI 2** sit on a pair of stools. **SHIKIGAMI 1** holds a gigantic book in her arms, a ledger of some kind. **SHIKIGAMI 2** has a pencil behind his ear. They watch **GINGER** and smile.)*

SHIKIGAMI 1 & 2. You're a lovely dancer.

GINGER. Stop it.

SHIKIGAMI 1 & 2. Ayuh. It's gonna' go wonderfully.

GINGER. How do I look?

SHIKIGAMI 1. Ginger, ya' look cunnin'.

SHIKIGAMI 2. Wicked cunnin', Ginger.

GINGER. You always say that. She's late.

SHIKIGAMI 1. There's traffic [tonight.]

SHIKIGAMI 2. [Traffic is] just numb. What can [you do?]

SHIKIGAMI 1. [Or maybe] she got lost on [the way.]

SHIKIGAMI 2. [You're not] the best with directions.

(GINGER stops singing to herself, stops dancing.)

GINGER. So it's my fault?

SHIKIGAMI 1 & 2. No.

SHIKIGAMI 2. But…

*(He looks at **SHIKIGAMI 1**. She opens the giant book across her lap. And puts her finger to the page.)*

SHIKIGAMI 1. On April 11, 1962 ya' gave a woman directions to meet ya' at a speakeasy in Olympia, Washington and she was lost for hours because of one-way streets ya' didn't mention and attacked by troublemakers.

SHIKIGAMI 2. On January 22, 1931 ya' abandoned a woman in a giant hedge maze just outside of Concord, New Hampshire because ya' were running ahead apiece, ahead too fast, and she got lost.

SHIKIGAMI 1. And it's cold in January in New Hampshire.

SHIKIGAMI 2. I miss the cold.

SHIKIGAMI 1. I miss the north.

SHIKIGAMI 2. On May 6, 1989 ya' told a woman in Rockford, Illinois the best way to get to your [house was...]

GINGER. [Okay, Jesus,] fine. So I'm bad with directions. Fine.

(**SHIKIGAMI 1 & 2** *exchange a satisfied glance as* **SHIKI-GAMI 2** *closes the giant book.*)

I hate that book. And anyway, this is different. How could you not find this hotel? It doesn't look like anything else in the entire city.

SHIKIGAMI 1. I'm sure you're right. Maybe you should have a piece of chocolate. That always calms you down.

GINGER. Ugh, that would be delicious. But I didn't bring any. I didn't want it to melt in my purse.

SHIKIGAMI 2. Then maybe ya' should take another Xanax.

GINGER. I've already had 3. Ugh, blind dates are so nerve racking.

SHIKIGAMI 1 & 2. Don't get gawmy; it's not your first blind date.

(**SHIKIGAMI 1** *begins to open the book for reference.*)

GINGER. Close that book now. I know it's not my first. It's technically number 476. The more women change, the more they stay the same.

SHIKIGAMI 1 & 2. Well let's try and be a little more upbeat.

SHIKIGAMI 1. If you can get this one to work.

SHIKIGAMI 2. Any of them, just get any of them [to work.]

SHIKIGAMI 1. [Ayuh, any] of them.

(*She gives* **SHIKIGAMI 2** *a sharp look. He looks back defiantly.*)

SHIKIGAMI 2. Don't look at me like that. I want to go back up north. Where it's cold. Where the night sky is crisp and clear and makes you feel small but like you have a place. I'm tired of following her around.

(**GINGER** *puts her hands on her hips, annoyed.*)

SHIKIGAMI 2. *(cont.)* That's right, I'm tired of following ya' around. We do everything we can to help, to make this happen for ya', because your curse happens to come with perks.

SHIKIGAMI 1. He doesn't mean it.

SHIKIGAMI 2. I do, yes I do.

GINGER. It's not my fault that I'm this weird spirit thing; it's not my fault I'm not allowed to rest.

SHIKIGAMI 1 & 2. Ya' it is.

GINGER. Fine. Whatever, so maybe I wronged a woman. Once.

SHIKIGAMI 1 & 2. Ya' you did.

GINGER. A really, really long time ago. But does this feel like a reasonable punishment?

SHIKIGAMI 1 & 2. Ya' it does.

GINGER. Well, color me surprised.

SHIKIGAMI 2. And we're stuck followin' ya'.

SHIKIGAMI 1. It isn't gonna help at all for ya to get all out [of sorts.]

SHIKIGAMI 2. [Stuck followin'] ya' here of all places; I don't like this place.

SHIKIGAMI 1. Me either.

GINGER. I didn't ask for [your help.]

SHIKIGAMI 2. [And you're] drawn to this creepy hotel so we're drawn with ya'. Tethered to ya', dragged around, isn't that the finest kind? Creepy place after creepy place, can ya' imagine? And we're polite and we try to steer ya' back towards humanity, or at least peace, but you're so stubborn, ya' never listen, ya never [take heed.]

SHIKIGAMI 1. [Ayuh, now] this [isn't gonna...]

SHIKIGAMI 2. [Ya' won't] even look at the book. Ya' know you can learn from your past mistakes, that's the whole point [of the...]

SHIKIGAMI 1. [Why don't] we all just calm it down, all right? It takes one true love and none of us have to do this anymore. Then we can head back north, finally, and ya' can go on where you like or wherever you go next. Easy as that, right?

SHIKIGAMI 2. *(under his breath...)* Except you keep eating all of them.

(GINGER turns on them sharply.)

GINGER. What?

SHIKIGAMI 1. He didn't say [anything.]

SHIKIGAMI 2. [I didn't say] anything.

GINGER. It's not my fault that I get hungry. That's not my fault. You don't understand the hunger, you won't listen when I try to explain it, the [way it...]

SHIKIGAMI 2. [Excuses.]

SHIKIGAMI 1. Stop it.

GINGER. It's just this thing that happens, when I get even a little bit excited. My heart pounds so hard, I smell flowers or some kind of, and then it happens before I even know what I'm doing, my mouth waters and my teeth itch and I'm just tearing away at their soft flesh, I have no idea why it's so hard, but it is and there's nothing I can do but try to do the right thing. Again and again. I just wish I were better at it.

(Something in her becomes more menacing.)

And I'm sorry if you're getting impatient, I'm sorry you have to follow me around, trust me, and I'm sorry if my damnation is getting wearisome for you, fuck off. Now, I have a solid feeling about this one, I'm feeling very "in control" so stop agitating me. If you want to help me make this happen then just lay off.

SHIKIGAMI 1. We know it's not your fault; it's part of the deal.

(SHIKIGAMI 2 taps the book in SHIKIGAMI 1's lap.)

SHIKIGAMI 2. But this? This is a wicked high number of women you've eaten.

SHIKIGAMI 1. Consumed.

SHIKIGAMI 2. Eaten. Your skin turns white, your jaw goes all gawmy, it's terrifyin' and you're lucky ya' don't have to see it. But we do. So if you want to…

(**SHIKIGAMI 2** *abruptly stops as both* **SHIKIGAMIS** *notice* **VIOLET** *enter.* **GINGER** *turns. They take each other in cautiously.*)

VIOLET. Ginger?

GINGER. Violet?

VIOLET. Yes.

GINGER. Oh good. I mean, good to meet you. That sounded funny, ugh. Not good like "oh good you're not ugly." Oh! But you're not ugly, not at all, I mean you're very nice and I'm just going to stop right now because I am not doing well at all with this whole first impression thing, am I?

(*pause*)

I'm glad you came.

VIOLET. Me too. Although, honestly, I thought about not showing up.

GINGER. Oh.

VIOLET. Dancing?

GINGER. They have these impromptu things, in hotel ballrooms all over town. It seemed like a good icebreaker, I don't know.

VIOLET. Well here I am, even though I haven't danced in a long time, don't even know if I remember how anymore. Sorry.

GINGER. Ah.

VIOLET. But, but I absolutely wanted to meet you.

GINGER. That's good.

VIOLET. I've heard such good things.

GINGER. Have you?

VIOLET. Just the other thing, the dancing thing…

> *(She trails off, taking an awkward step away from* **GINGER.***)*

GINGER. Well, I don't want you to be uncomfortable or [anything.]

VIOLET. [And I] really appreciate that.

GINGER. But there will be dancing in there. I know, I know, why don't I show you a few simple steps before we go in, okay, just out [here?]

VIOLET. [Oh no,] you don't have to do that, it's [really…]

> *(***GINGER** *moves in, forcing* **VIOLET** *into a dance position.)*

GINGER. [Oh hush,] it'll be fun, come on.

VIOLET. I don't really know [what to…]

GINGER. [Shhhh. Just] follow me. You'll be great.

> *(***GINGER** *moves* **VIOLET** *around, slowly shifting into a dance.* **GINGER** *hums a tune for them. It becomes a song, a lovely song, beautiful and hypnotic. They giggle and swap quick glances as* **VIOLET** *slowly becomes less clumsy with a simple step. This takes a moment and is crushed under excruciating anticipation.)*

VIOLET. I think I'm getting it.

GINGER. Look at you. See, it's not hard.

> *(They laugh. Then stop, caught in a moment, very close. The* **SHIKIGAMIS** *hold each other's hands in excitement.* **VIOLET** *breaks.)*

VIOLET. Sorry.

GINGER. I'm sorry.

VIOLET. Oh no, no, don't you be sorry.

GINGER. No?

VIOLET. It's okay, really. I didn't mean to…

GINGER. All right.

VIOLET. You're so, I don't mind saying, there's something so compelling about you and…I'm just a little rusty.

GINGER. You were doing great.

VIOLET. No.

GINGER. You really were. You're…great.

VIOLET. Thank you.

GINGER. You…you smell like flowers. Oh, it's so ridiculous, I feel like a little girl.

VIOLET. Me too, [it's so…]

GINGER. [Would] you, Violet I know this sounds, and I don't want to be, but you just, oh, good grief, Violet, after the party, if we have a good time I mean, would you want to grab some dinner?

(The **SHIKIGAMIS** *exchange a worried look.)*

Here in the hotel. You can really work up an appetite dancing.

*(***VIOLET** *lights up and then tries to hide it. The* **SHIKI-GAMIS** *both lean forward on their stools and whisper urgently to* **GINGER.***)*

SHIKIGAMI 1. Don't do it.

SHIKIGAMI 2. She's nice.

VIOLET. I don't see why not.

GINGER. Oh.

VIOLET. Yes.

GINGER. Well, okay. Let's dance.

VIOLET. And…we don't have to stay long.

*(***GINGER** *smiles. She takes* **VIOLET***'s hand.)*

SHIKIGAMI 1 & 2. Please be nice.

(As the women leave the circle, **GINGER** *looks back…)*

GINGER. I'll do my best.

(She exits with a little wave.)

*(***SHIKIGAMI 1** *sighs and opens the gigantic book.* **SHIKIGAMI 2** *pulls the pencil from behind his ear and, shaking his head, he crosses out something in the book.)*

End Scene

vi. a personal account
of the renovation

(Lights up on **FRANKLIN** *in a smart tie. He is standing alone in the circle, off center. He waits, hands crossed, perhaps whistling.)*

(Just outside of the circle, barely lit, the **OBAKE** *sits in a chair. Her legs crossed. She listens attentively holding a simple desk bell in her lap.)*

(A man enters, a hotel **GUEST** *with an overnight bag. He stops to yawn and rubs his eyes.)*

FRANKLIN. Good evening, sir.

GUEST. Hello.

FRANKLIN. Or morning, it is quite late. Coming aboard?

GUEST. Yes, I…yes.

(He enters the elevator. They stand for a moment and the **GUEST** *looks about awkwardly.)*

FRANKLIN. What floor?

GUEST. Oh, right. Right. 11.

FRANKLIN. Ah, good floor.

GUEST. 11?

FRANKLIN. Mm hm, it's just high enough to see over some of the other buildings.

*(**FRANKLIN** presses an unseen button with his fingertip.)*

GUEST. No lever?

FRANKLIN. Oh, no, just the buttons.

GUEST. Seems so old fashioned to have an elevator operator.

FRANKLIN. Actually I'm a concierge. Franklin Mims. I have my master's degree in hospitality administration, but we all take shifts in the elevator. Part of ensuring the "luxury experience" for our guests.

GUEST. God forbid we should have to push our own buttons.

*(**FRANKLIN** looks at him, a look devoid of anything.)*

Kinda' slow, huh?

(The light dims some as the doors close.)

FRANKLIN. The owners feel that having service in the elevators creates a certain kind of atmosphere, that kind of thing. And, you know, makes up for all of those stories about this place.

GUEST. Stories?

FRANKLIN. You don't know about the, ah, I see, well just ignore the stories. There are only the two elevators, east and west, just the two, so that's not much more to staff I suppose.

GUEST. And this is…?

FRANKLIN. I'm always east, sir. Two elevators, 14 floors. I'm always east.

GUEST. 14 floors, that's a good size. You said you're name's Franklin?

FRANKLIN. Franklin Mims. I prefer Ms. Mims though.

GUEST. Ms?

FRANKLIN. Professional courtesy, if you don't mind.

GUEST. No, it's just, I wanted to make sure I heard you correctly when…

*(A bell sounds. It is the **OBAKE** ringing the desk bell.)*

FRANKLIN. 8.

*(And the doors open. **CANARY**, bloodied and beaten, literally drags himself into the elevator.)*

GUEST. Jesus. Jesus, are you all [right.]

CANARY. [Get the fuck] away from me!

GUEST. This man needs help.

FRANKLIN. He lives in the hotel. Best to leave it alone, sir.

*(The doors close as the **CANARY** cowers in the corner. Quickly and quietly he recites a rhyme to himself. It's barely audible…)*

CANARY. Mary had a pretty bird
　　　feathers bright and yellow
　　　slender legs, upon my word
　　　he was a pretty fellow
　　　Mary had a pretty bird
　　　feathers bright and yellow

GUEST. Do, do you [need…]

CANARY. [Leave me alone!]

GUEST. I'm sorry, I [didn't…]

FRANKLIN. [Sir, please] don't disturb the other guests.

GUEST. Franklin, I'm [trying to…]

FRANKLIN. [Ms. Mims,] if you don't mind.

(*The* GUEST *takes a step away from* CANARY *as he begins to whimper.*)

CANARY. Feathers bright and yellow.
　　　Feathers bright and yellow.

FRANKLIN. You know, this is the original elevator system, the mechanics I mean, the guts of it. They updated the interface, but all the rest is authentic. Some people think the elevators are haunted, but I don't put much stock in it. Some people think the hotel is haunted, but that's…

(*The bell sounds again.*)

12.

GUEST. We missed my floor.

FRANKLIN. Sir, with all due respect, I don't tell you how to do your job.

(*And the doors open.* PUNCH *enters wearing an apron. She has a thick, syrupy Southern accent.*)

PUNCH. Franklin.

FRANKLIN. Ms. Punch.

CANARY. No, no.

PUNCH. Oh, yes.

CANARY. I'm not a bird.

PUNCH. Now honey, where did you think you were runnin', little Canary?

CANARY. I'm not a bird.

PUNCH. A little bird.

CANARY. I'm not a bird.

PUNCH. My little bird.

CANARY. And often where the cage was hung
 And often where the cage was hung
 And often where the cage [was hung]

PUNCH. [Shut the] fuck up! Now, are we done yet, little Canary?

CANARY. I can only do this so many [times.]

PUNCH. [Did I do] somethin' to make you think we were all finished up, little Canary? No I did not. Now, be still. 17 please.

GUEST. 17?

(*PUNCH spins and slaps the* **GUEST** *hard, knocking him back.*)

PUNCH. Trust me when I tell you, sugar, it's better not to speak.

(**FRANKLIN** *pushes a button with his fingertip. They all stand awkwardly for a moment,* **PUNCH** *rubbing* **CANARY**'s *hair as he cowers, the* **GUEST** *holding his face. The doors close. The* **GUEST** *leans over to* **FRANKLIN**…)

GUEST. Aren't you going to do something?

(**FRANKLIN** *begins whistling again. Then, a bell sounds again.*)

FRANKLIN. 23.

(*And the doors open. This time the light is filled with shadows. A painfully deafening combination of metal churning, things in motion and horrified screams fills the space. The* **GUEST**'s *eyes go wide with horror at whatever he sees outside and he presses to the back of the circle. The other people in the elevator pay it no mind. The* **GUEST** *is hyperventilating. He crumples onto* *the floor covering his eyes.* **PUNCH** *examines her nails absent-mindedly.* **CANARY** *tries to get up, but she smacks him. The doors close.*)

FRANKLIN. *(cont.)* There was a great deal of hubbub when the hotel was being renovated you know? They still talk about it, people protesting from the local community foundation complaining about maintaining the original architecture and people from neighboring buildings complaining that the added height would ruin their views. They only added a few floors and it looks like it was always this way, doesn't it? Just like part of the original design. Frankly, I'm amazed at how quickly they got the project done in the end. You know, they even got the original architect to sign off on the renovations in order to quiet those historical critics. It wasn't easy because he's a crazy old man now, crazy, but it lends the whole undertaking a bit more artistic credibility somehow.

(A bell sounds again.)

17.

(And the doors open. **PUNCH** *drags* **CANARY** *out of the elevator.)*

PUNCH. Goodnight, Franklin.

(The doors close.)

GUEST. Oh my god.

FRANKLIN. It's terrifying isn't it? Keeping a bird as a pet, I hate birds, especially large birds, but it takes all kinds, doesn't it?

GUEST. Oh my god.

FRANKLIN. You're right though, about the elevators, they are quite slow and a bit unpredictable. Between you and me, most of the staff would prefer they rip out the insides of these old things and just go for it, go completely modern. Can you imagine? Just tear them out all together, a full evisceration, you know?

GUEST. I think I'm going to be sick.

FRANKLIN. Cleave the building open and excise the elevator cars, drag every piece of cable and steel out, pull on it until it snaps, gives way, or sever the stubborn parts, get a nice, firm grip and just wrench it all out. Doesn't seem like it's going to happen though. A shame since they did all this construction on the outside. Do you know the name of the architect? I should know, I think he was famous.

(*pause*)

I'll have to ask someone next time I think about it.

GUEST. The lobby.

FRANKLIN. I'm sorry?

GUEST. The lobby, I want to…go, go to the lobby.

(*A bell sounds.*)

FRANKLIN. Oh, but here we are at 11.

GUEST. What?

(*The doors open. The* GUEST *stays crumpled up.* FRANKLIN *reaches a hand out to his shoulder. The* GUEST *jerks away.* FRANKLIN *picks up the* GUEST*'s bag and holds it out. The* GUEST *takes it and crawls out of the elevator.*)

FRANKLIN. Enjoy your stay, sir.

End Scene

vii. above ground

(**DAVID** *stands in the circle nervously looking at his watch. He is dressed to impress, adjusting his tie in a nervous repetition. Checks his watch again. He is obviously in public view, probably up on a dais of some kind.*)

(**SIMONE** *enters. She is dressed simple and chic with a small clutch purse. Approaching, she smoothes out her dress.*)

DAVID. Where have you been?

SIMONE. I'm sorry.

DAVID. They were taking all of these photos. Until they realized you weren't here.

SIMONE. I said I'm sorry.

DAVID. Nobody even knows who I am.

SIMONE. Everyone knows who you are.

DAVID. Well they want photos of the architect's granddaughter, not her husband.

SIMONE. They let me do one last walk through and I got a little lost.

DAVID. It is a big building.

(They look out at the building in question.)

Still seems like a shame to demolish it.

SIMONE. A Buck Mason triumph. But the foundation is collapsing. The ground underneath it is giving away.

DAVID. Still, it's a shame.

SIMONE. I hurt my wrist.

DAVID. How?

SIMONE. I don't know. Lifting or, I don't know. Somewhere in the hotel. I took something though; it'll be fine soon.

DAVID. Simone. Today?

SIMONE. I took something for the pain. You don't want me to stand through this hurting do you? And…also something for my nerves. That's all.

DAVID. Look at me.

(She does.)

You're about to go all glassy, aren't [you?]

SIMONE. [I told you,] I only took the two things. And maybe something to relax.

DAVID. Something for pain. Something for nerves. Something to relax.

SIMONE. Who can remember, just stop it, I'm fine. It's his most famous hotel. And it's going to be parking; did you know that?

DAVID. You've mentioned it 20 or 30 [times.]

SIMONE. [From] near majesty to parking.

DAVID. Like I said, it's a shame.

SIMONE. I was a little girl in that building. My grandfather made sure everyone knew exactly who I was when we would visit. His favorite little girl running around his most stunningly successful design.

DAVID. It's funny.

SIMONE. Hmm?

DAVID. You never talk about your childhood.

SIMONE. I'm feeling this overwhelming nostalgia.

DAVID. That's not nostalgia; it's the pills. Now, where is the old man anyway?

SIMONE. Around I'm sure. Just look for the clutch of photographers.

DAVID. I haven't seen him since this [morning.]

SIMONE. [Well he] wouldn't miss this David. He's here somewhere. You know, he had them move the entire hotel over from its original footprint? After they started construction, concrete already poured, he had them move the entire thing just a little bit to the side.

DAVID. Why?

SIMONE. Eccentricity?

DAVID. Huh.

SIMONE. I used to go up with him when his buildings were under construction. They'd strap this white hard hat on me and let me walk around on the open girders, seriously just one foot in front of the other into open space.

DAVID. You're kidding?

SIMONE. Nope. I was six or seven. In an over-sized hard hat. My grandfather let me do anything I wanted to really.

DAVID. You'd never get me up there like that.

SIMONE. Oh you are not afraid of heights. [Come on.]

DAVID. [No, no, not] heights. As long as there's glass and steel and all of the things that keep you on the inside, I'm fine. But being out in the open like that where you could just fall. That's crazy. I might have a heart attack just thinking about it, I mean really imagining it. It's terrifying.

SIMONE. Maybe. But I loved it.

DAVID. I'm happy right here on the ground thank you very much. Seriously, the old man is late.

SIMONE. It doesn't really matter. They'll do it without him.

DAVID. You think?

SIMONE. They're supposed to do it at sunset, no matter what. Just boom and then a cloud of dust and...

(She is dizzy for a moment, leaning on DAVID.)

DAVID. Whoa, here you go. Come on. Stand up.

SIMONE. I'm standing up. Don't worry, they'll just, just think I'm over-emotional.

(She regains her footing.)

DAVID. Something for pain, something for nerves, something [to relax.]

SIMONE. [Well it's] a big day.

DAVID. Are you all right?

(She laughs coldly looking at the hotel. He looks out at the building as well. They do not look at each other.)

SIMONE. Hotel hotel [hotel hotel…]

DAVID. [I wish we] could have made it through one day. I thought since we'd be out in public, literally having our pictures taken, I thought we might make it through one day. I'm a, I'm a patient guy, but it's getting worse, Simone.

SIMONE. No.

DAVID. Yes.

SIMONE. Maybe.

(pause)

DAVID. Look, okay, I know today is stressful, I know it. And I'm here with you because I said I would be and I want to be. I do. But you really need to try and stay as clear headed as possible, okay? Especially if your grandfather is one of his moods, I need you on my side and together.

SIMONE. I'm focusing.

DAVID. When he gets all crazy, he's a handful all by himself, all that babble about ghosts under the floor, in the ground and whatever. I can't deal with both of you spacing out. So just…don't take anything else until after they blow up the building, all right?

SIMONE. I think I'll be doing much better in the very near future. The sun is almost down.

DAVID. Ugh, what difference does that make?

SIMONE. "Droit de seigneur."

DAVID. You know I don't speak French.

SIMONE. Yes.

DAVID. I hate when you do that.

SIMONE. It's a phrase my grandfather taught me. It means 'the lord's right.' And in medieval times it, oh David, do you ever wish there was just one thing, some kind of, just a single thing we could blame for all of the other horrible things in life?

DAVID. No.

SIMONE. Wouldn't it make everything, not everything, but the bad things, easier to accept if there was some kind of awful volition to all of it?

DAVID. I seriously doubt it.

SIMONE. I don't know, I just, do you want to hear a story about this hotel?

DAVID. You're not even making sense now, Simone.

SIMONE. Do you want to hear a secret story about this hotel?

DAVID. Not if it's a long story.

SIMONE. After my father and mother went away, died I guess, but really they just vanished. After that I did everything with my grandfather. When he would bring me here, and I was just a little girl then, he would always come into my room at night to tuck me in. And he would tell me a story. Never at home, only when we came here.

DAVID. Can we please just [try to...]

SIMONE. [It was] a story about a bright and handsome young man who made a deal with some horrible thing in order to gain a single wish. And he wished for a beautiful girl. And his wish was granted.

(She puts the back of her hand over her mouth for a moment as if struggling to keep something down. She still looks at the hotel.)

And then he would kiss me goodnight. I mean to say David that he would kiss me goodnight in a way that no little girl should ever be kissed. This man that I trusted, the only man in the world, with hands like oil spilling onto my body. Wet and dirty.

DAVID. Oh my god.

SIMONE. Only at this hotel. He said, and it didn't make any sense at the time, he said he got to have me first. At seven years old, he got to have me first.

DAVID. Simone.

SIMONE. "Droit de seigneur."

DAVID. How do I, how do I not know this?

SIMONE. *(coolly wiping away a few tears)* Now don't get all worked up. Why is that something you'd know? I don't even want to know it; I certainly don't want other people to know it. But something about today [and the...]

(DAVID quickly looks around, scanning the crowd.)

DAVID. [Where is] he now, right now?

SIMONE. Why?

DAVID. You were just a little girl.

SIMONE. I was just a little girl.

DAVID. You were just a little girl!

SIMONE. Oh David, it all happened so long ago. There's nothing you can do, what are you going to do if you find him?

DAVID. I don't, I don't know. Something.

SIMONE. In front of all these people? The reporters and photographers?

DAVID. In front of these, I don't care, yes! I don't care who sees me, Simone. He hurt you? You're telling me he hurt you? I'll break every bone in his old, decaying body.

SIMONE. *(rubbing her wrist again, turning her hand around and around)* Can you believe they let me wander around that building before the demolition? It seems so dangerous, so many heavy things. And monsters. Can you imagine?

DAVID. Where is he?

SIMONE. It's finally going to be over, David.

DAVID. Where is he?

SIMONE. Bleeding from the head. Unconscious. In room 728.

(The sound of an explosion rings out and a brief blast of light flickers across the two. SIMONE's face registers delight, even wonder, with a smile and a small gasp.)

(**DAVID** *slowly turns to look at her as the building is erased.*)

End Scene

epilogue

(**DAVID** *turns again to look at the building. He slowly reaches out and takes* **SIMONE***'s hand. She does not look away from the blast site.*)

(*The* **OBAKE** *steps into the circle as the rest of the ensemble joins* **DAVID** *and* **SIMONE***. They all look towards the collapsed building and then, slowly, their gaze drifts towards the* **OBAKE***. She smiles and nods.*)

(**BUCK** *collapses into the circle as the lights dim.*)

(*The rest of the ensemble scatters as he crashes to the ground. They move behind the* **OBAKE** *and form the* **MASS** *again.*)

(**BUCK** *slowly tries to rise, but can't get to his feet. He's a much older man now, his life is behind him. He has a head injury again. Fresh. He struggles to produce a pair of spectacles from his pocket and get them on. The* **MASS** *hisses and releases a low moan.* **BUCK** *turns to see the* **OBAKE** *and, startled, pushes himself away a bit.*)

OBAKE. Oh, there you are, Buck Mason.

(*The* **OBAKE** *offers him a little wave.*)

Welcome back.

END OF PLAY

OTHER TITLES AVAILABLE FROM SAMUEL FRENCH

OCTOPUS

Steve Yockey

Dark Comedy / 5m / Unit set

After young couple Kevin and Blake engage in an adventurous and hastily planned night of group sex with the older, more "experienced" Max and Andy, they are left trying to salvage their relationship from a pummeling mix of jealousy, betrayal, telegrams from a soaking wet delivery boy and a ravenous sea monster from the ocean floor. This universal love story rendered through a post-modern gay lens slips from domestic comedy into a darkly fantastic fable examining the role and depth of commitment in relationships and what it really means to say the words "I love you."

"A fiercely imaginative and finely tuned new voice... Smartly observed and blissfully performed... *Octopus'* tentacles tickle the funny bone, awake the mind and tug on the heart."
– *San Francisco Chronicle*

"An evening full of arresting images… classic tragedy seen through a very contemporary ironic lens"
– *Marin Independent Journal*

"This tale of two gay couples' group sex fling and its serious consequences arrives at a powerful statement about illness and love."
– *Variety*

SAMUELFRENCH.COM

SAMUEL FRENCH STAFF

Nate Collins
President

Ken Dingledine
Director of Operations,
Vice President

Bruce Lazarus
Executive Director,
General Counsel

Rita Maté
Director of Finance

ACCOUNTING

Lori Thimsen | Director of Licensing Compliance
Nehal Kumar | Senior Accounting Associate
Helena Mezzina | Royalty Administration
Glenn Halcomb | Royalty Administration
Jessica Zheng | Accounts Receivable
Andy Lian | Accounts Payable
Charlie Sou | Accounting Associate
Joann Mannello | Orders Administrator

CUSTOMER SERVICE AND LICENSING

Brad Lohrenz | Director of Licensing Development
Laura Lindson | Licensing Services Manager
Kim Rogers | Theatrical Specialist
Matthew Akers | Theatrical Specialist
Ashley Byrne | Theatrical Specialist
Jennifer Carter | Theatrical Specialist
Annette Storckman | Theatrical Specialist
Dyan Flores | Theatrical Specialist
Sarah Weber | Theatrical Specialist
Nicholas Dawson | Theatrical Specialist
Andrew Clarke | Theatrical Specialist
David Kimple | Theatrical Specialist

EDITORIAL

Amy Rose Marsh | Literary Manager
Ben Coleman | Editorial Associate
Caitlin Bartow | Assistant to the Executive Director

MARKETING

Abbie Van Nostrand | Director of Corporate
     Communications
Ryan Pointer | Marketing Manager
Courtney Kochuba | Marketing Associate

PUBLICATIONS AND PRODUCT DEVELOPMENT

Joe Ferreira | Product Development Manager
David Geer | Publications Manager
Charlyn Brea | Publications Associate
Tyler Mullen | Publications Associate
Derek P. Hassler | Musical Products Coordinator
Zachary Orts | Musical Materials Coordinator

OPERATIONS

Casey McLain | Operations Supervisor
Elizabeth Minski | Office Coordinator, Reception
Coryn Carson | Office Coordinator, Reception

SAMUEL FRENCH BOOKSHOP (LOS ANGELES)

Joyce Mehess | Bookstore Manager
Cory DeLair | Bookstore Buyer
Jennifer Palumbo | Bookstore Order Dept. Manager
Sonya Wallace | Bookstore Associate
Tim Coultas | Bookstore Associate
Alfred Contreras | Shipping & Receiving

LONDON OFFICE

Felicity Barks | Rights & Contracts Associate
Steve Blacker | Bookshop Associate
David Bray | Customer Services Associate
Zena Choi | Professional Licensing Associate
Robert Cooke | Assistant Buyer
Stephanie Dawson | Amateur Licensing Associate
Simon Ellison | Retail Sales Manager
Jason Felix | Royalty Administration
Susan Griffiths | Amateur Licensing Associate
Robert Hamilton | Amateur Licensing Associate
Lucy Hume | Publications Manager
Nasir Khan | Management Accountant
Simon Magniti | Royalty Administration
Louise Mappley | Amateur Licensing Associate
James Nicolau | Despatch Associate
Martin Phillips | Librarian
Zubayed Rahman | Despatch Associate
Steve Sanderson | Royalty Administration Supervisor
Douglas Schatz | Acting Executive Director
Roger Sheppard | I.T. Manager
Panos Panayi | Company Accountant
Peter Smith | Amateur Licensing Associate
Garry Spratley | Customer Service Manager
David Webster | UK Operations Director